I0677886

18

We believe... that the applause of silence is the only kind that counts.
—Alfred Jarry

BLACK SCAT review

Number 18

Dec. 2019

Black Scat Review, an international journal of the arts, is published irregularly—designed & produced in Northern California by merry elves. Copies are available for order in Europe & North America on Amazon and at a few select bookshops.

Editor: **Norman Conquest**

Copyright © 2019
All rights reserved.
ISBN-13 978-1-7331656-4-8

Cover: photograph by **Alexander Krivitskiy**
Facing page: photograph by **Jim McMenamin**
Back cover: photograph by **Farewell Debut**

ANTI-CONTENTS PAGE

Seek and ye shall find...

After a long hiatus, we return refreshed, in book form, sporting a new design, and an international roster of artists and writers. First, we bring Bohemian Paris to life with a blast of fresh air, i.e., translations of **Alfred Jarry, Arthur Rimbaud, Paul Verlaine, Théophile Gautier, Charles Cros, Laurent Tailhade**, and **Jules Jouy**—an extraordinary roundup of avant-garde souls. That alone would be worth the price of admission, but there's more! Fiction, art & poetry by an all-star cast of luminaries: **Mark Axelrod, Angela Buck, Peter Cherches, Norman Conquest, Catherine D'Avis, Farewell Debut, Eckhard Gerdes, Bob Heman, Charles Holdefer, Rhys Hughes, Esteban Isnardi, Harold Jaffe, Alexander Krivitskiy, Olchar E. Lindsann, Joel Lipman, Laura Mazzenga, Jim McMenamin, Peter McAdam, Doug Rice, Jason E. Rolfe, Paul Rosheim, Doug Skinner, Gregory Wallace**, and **Tom Whalen**.

So sink your teeth into the issue and enjoy.

COLOPHON

Visiting typeface: Vista Slab, designed by Xavier Dupré, *Emigre*.

Body text: Adobe Caslon designed by Carol Twombly

Titles: Adam.CG designed by Shrenik Ganatra

Headers: Italiana designed by Santiago Orozco

Black Scat Review

19

— theme —

e c s t a s y

Deadline:

March 31, 2020

Alfred Jarry

The

POPE'S MUSTARD-MAKER

A COMIC OPERETTA IN THREE ACTS

FIRST ENGLISH TRANSLATION

BLACK SCAT BOOKS

Drawn from Black Scat's eight editions of the master French absurdist, this compendium is a sublime introduction to the wordplay and black humor that shocked and dazzled Bohemian Paris in the raucous "Banquet Years." The READER includes the celebrated pataphysical text "A Thoroughly Parisian Drama"—a favorite of both André Breton and the Oulipians—as well as stories, plays, an excerpt from his only novel, and the classic exploits of Captain Cap and Francisque Sarcey. The translator, Doug Skinner, has added copious notes and an illuminating introduction. Step into the funhouse! Laughs and surprises await!

THE ALPHONSE ALLAIS READER
Compiled & Translated by Doug Skinner
182 pp., $14.95
Black Scat Books

an excerpt from

THE POPE'S MUSTARD-MAKER
A Comic Operetta in Three Acts

by Alfred Jarry

Translated from the French by Doug Skinner

ACT ONE

The pope's dressing room.

SCENE I

THE POPE, THE CHAMBERMAID, THE GRAND MUSTARD-MAKER, THE GRAND MULETEER, THE GRAND PAPER-MAKER, LITTLE MUSTARD-MAKERS OF THE SISTINE CHAPEL, VARIOUS DIGNITARIES.

(*The* POPE *is seated upstage on a sort of throne. The* CHAMBERMAID *dresses him.*)

CHORUS

O Rome! Embrace without restraint
Pope John the Eighth, our Holy Father!
Though he has what it takes to be a saint,
He must have what it takes to be a father.
We hope
We can
Show that the Pope's a man.
O Rome, embrace without restraint
The Holy Father!
Glory to the Holy Father!
Glory to the holy man!

THE MUSTARD-MAKER

I am the Mustard-Maker, chief of all,
Grand master of all ceremony,
The condiment of ceremony,

I call

For proper pomp and sanctimony.

I oversee the protocol.

I am the Mustard-Maker, chief of all.

The babbling rabble I suppress,

And say the time has come to dress

Without delay

The time, I say,

Our forces must be mustered, yes,

The time to dress

His Holiness!

A DIGNITARY

From the basilica we bear

The true tiara he must wear!

THE GRAND PAPER-MAKER

You are Peter,

On this rock

Place the keys of paradise,

One, two:

And only two, for two suffice.

Miserere, de profundis,

The keys of the Apostle Peter.

THE GRAND MULETEER

Here is, according to the rule,

The papal slipper, papal mule,

Wherein the foot must now be put.

It fits in this,

The foot we kiss!

Now ring your jingles, papal foot!

And dance according to the rules,

The caper of the papal mules!

CHORUS

You must not go

Too slow

And though the papal mules you wear

Make quite a pretty little pair,

A trot

Would not…

Oh no! A trot's the best you've got!

So ring your jingles, papal mules,

A gallop is the perfect thing

To make the holy jingles ring.

(*End of the dance of the mules.*)

THE CHAMBERMAID

He danced very well. This young pope is extraordinary.

THE GRAND MULETEER

The pope does everything very well; it's his job. He's infallible.

THE CHAMBERMAID

Everything! I don't think His Holiness permits himself everything. (*Sigh.*) He's not at all like his predecessors were with their nice big chambermaid! (*Sigh.*) His flesh is strong. But anyway, our young pope is charming, and not even a woman could have shown such lightness and grace.

ARIA

I

For he's more like a young popess
Than pope, as far as I can see.
And truth compels me to confess
I've had three popes who died… on me.
But he a virgin seems to be,
With rosy cheeks and beardless chin,
A prude who seems too cold to sin.
Is he a pope? Oh yes, unless
He's a popess?

II

And me, the secret chambermaid,
This pope so young and full of gloom
Avoids, and dodges to evade.

He's like a leper in his room,

A bride in hiding from her groom.

His hair is all he's shown me, and

When he says mass, his dainty hand.

Is he a pope? Oh yes, unless

He's a popess?

THE MUSTARD-MAKER

My girl, you might deserve excommunication! But, fortunately for you, you don't know what you're saying. No woman can enter the conclave of cardinals, and it's already too much to tolerate a chambermaid here. Many years have passed since those absurd legends of popesses. In our century of progress, the ninth century, the ceremony we're preparing is truly superfluous.

THE CHAMBERMAID

Ah yes, the Chair!

THE MUSTARD-MAKER

I say superfluous, but as Grand Mustard-Maker, that is, grand master of all ceremony, I must see to it that the more superfluous all formalities are, the better they be observed.

ARIA

The Chair,

As you're aware,
Is a very sacred spot:
The seat,
The Holy Seat,
Sanctioned by the Sacred College,
Where the Pope will squat.

And it's a nimbus, it's a hat,
A halo worn around the rear,
It's like the hoop an acrobat
Has trained her little horse to clear.

For I must tell you, soul to soul,
The chair is fitted with a hole,
A frame of true virility,
Of true infallibility.

And we'll see if the Holy Father
Has what it takes to be a father.
The Chair,
As you're aware (*etc.*)
(*The chorus repeats the refrain. General exit. The* POPESS
and MUSTARD-MAKER *remain.*)

[End of Scene One]

UN CAP'F AMOUREX

Doug Rice

A decade or so after October 13, 1960, Saint Mary's Church would burn to the ground. The parishioners would stand and stare at the flames. Some would cry and say that the flames went as high as the heavens. They would say that the flames looked angry and wanted to burn the heavens away; others would whisper that a few of the parishioners themselves burst into flames and died begging for forgiveness. Others, it was said, melted. Those who survived and stood like marble statues watching the flames devour the house of their faith that day claimed the fire burned into the earth and all of the ashes disappeared; only a hole would remain, a gateway into Dante's deepest level of hell. Nothing good could rise from such an abyss. In bars up and down Butler Street in Sharpsburg, in Etna, in Lawrenceville, even as far away as the North Side, men and women alike spread tales of those who stared down into this hole going blind and losing their power of speech. Nothing, not even charred wood from the cross or broken concrete or marble remained. Saint Mary's Church was erased. Clouds fell from the sky, landed softly on the earth and turned into ashes. A few people told stories of the fire being so intense that it set the Allegheny River aflame; the waters of the river burned bright for seven days and seven nights. All that truly remained of Saint Mary's were these stories. To this day, many swear the fire is still burning beneath the ground where a new church—The Church of Holy Resurrection—was built ten years after the fire. A phoenix church rising from flames. A rebirth. Born again. But sins live forever, even though at times they seem to sleep and seem to be forgotten. Fire cannot burn away the marks of sin. Priests can only hope to forgive the sins of their parishioners. But they have no true belief that they can redeem their own souls from their own sins. It would be better to forget God.

Priests made pilgrimages from parishes all over the world and from all sorts of denominations to pray or meditate at the edge of the hole, to beg God or Allah or Buddha to forgive whatever caused this fire and to protect those families that continued to live in the small village of Sharpsburg. Even atheists came to stare into absolute nothingness. To see the emptiness of the nothingness that they believed in. To see what awaited them upon their death. A few of these atheists became believers, but they could not clearly say what they had begun believing; many believers did more than question their faith after seeing such a hole in the earth. Many retreated from the hole, walking backwards never taking their eyes away from the hole, transfixed as if at any moment it would burst into flames again. When they returned to the safety of their homes, they tore pages out of their Bibles and burned them. But the sins of the father can never be burned. Over the years before The Church of Holy Resurrection was built, twelve children fell or leapt into the abyss. Disappeared. Floated into the eternal depths. Laughing the whole way down, joyous, until the sound of their childish voices could no longer be heard by a living soul.

One firefighter would die fighting the fire, two others would be injured; the arson and insurance investigators would report that the fire was of "an indeterminate origin"; the cause, they claimed, could never truly be known. Not in this lifetime. "The fire," these official reports concluded, "had appeared out of nowhere." But Father Joseph would know the truth. The fire was an act of God, not nature, not arson, not flaws in electrical design. Beyond a shadow of a doubt those flames had risen directly from the depths of hell and had been sent to torment him. He knew God was as angry as Satan, and he knew such anger and bitter disappointment had no bounds. And God, most likely, was less forgiving than Satan. God demanded that people confess their sins, that they beg for redemption, that they do penance. When people disappointed Satan, he forgave them without punishing them.

The day of the fire, Father Joseph watched the flames licking the walls of Saint Mary's, setting the Holy Tabernacle and altar aflame. He wanted to celebrate the wisdom of God's bitterness, of His disappointment in him, of God's quirky expression of His love for mankind. This fire was sent for all Father Joseph had done and for all he would continue to do. There are no saints without a past and no sinners without a future. Father Joseph knew this and felt this spiteful fire had come to destroy what remained of his soul and of his memory of his mother. "Your father did things to me in the dark," Joseph's mother told him. "Things I enjoyed and things I will always remember and will never be able to forget. And now you are here with me. And I cannot forgive a man who did all that and then disappeared." His mother told him bedtime stories, night after night. "Your father spit out more sand than truth and nightly prayed for rain, for floods. God was jealous of your father."

Even on this day, decades before the fire, Father Joseph's soul was blackened and wounded by desperate years of longing. Each morning he woke a little more uncertain of the possibility of loving his neighbors or of forgiving those lonely bowed heads sitting in the dark, begging, in his confessional. He despised his neighbors as he feigned forgiveness upon their foreheads. Their loud music blaring out their windows at all hours of the day and night. The husband washing his car in ways that his wife wished he touched her. Other men standing, shirtless, on street corners complaining about the humidity in the summer and, bundled up inside parkas and tossle caps complaining about freezing rain, and frigid temperatures and wives in the winter. Mrs. Gilbert, mother of two or three children, wife of a muscular man who was little more than a heap of broken promises, always too obvious with bringing homemade cookies to Father Joseph that were not cookies at all. They were metaphors even to a blind man. Sitting in his rectory crossing and uncrossing her legs. Claiming to desire redemption. Mrs. Gilbert's evil eyes. Her curled lip. Her wanton kneecaps and earlobes. Twisting her wedding band as if it were diseased and burning through her skin. Wanting to be punished. Father Joseph sat trembling in his aloneness, staring at her breasts, starting at her knees. Deceitful, wicked and unjust. A woman weeping over her desires. And a priest tormented both by her tears and by his own tears as he stood and walked from behind his desk to her. It would not be the first time that he pulled a woman's hair and let sweat drip from his forehead onto a woman's forehead. It would not be the first time that he took revenge on a God who spoke in tongues mixing memory and desire, forgetting and forgiving mothers and fathers. Nor would it be the last time.

Each morning Father Joseph doubted the solemn truth of his own flesh. He lifted the body and blood of Christ between two fingers but doubted the communion. He knew God had looked away on the evening of his birth, that he was not made in the image of God. More likely, he created God in his own image for his own needs. Still, each morning he prayed for forgiveness of sins he had not yet committed. He burned for peace. He had only known isolation and unhappiness as a child. His mother abandoned him before he uttered his first words. She left him, naked and crying in a cardboard box, on the steps of the Sisters of the Immaculate Heart convent. Nuns rescued him. They hid him inside their bedrooms in the convent. They hid the small boy under their beds, in nooks and corners, beneath the stairwell, in the basement, and in closets. They fed and clothed him. They educated him. They named him and told him stories of his origins. He believed their words. They put their hand over his mouth when he cried. They told him to be quiet; they told him to not speak, only to listen. They told him his body would come to know more than his words could ever express. When he grew too large to remain hidden in the convent away from Sister Superior and the priests, Sister Regina took him to the Cranston Family on Perrysville Avenue, and Joseph became their son. Not in blood. In words.

They gave him permission to speak and cry and laugh. They tickled him. They spanked him. Then they tickled him again. They became his mother and father, and he came to learn that they loved the awkward mixture of tears and laughter. He could only speak of what was absent from his life. No one knew how old he was. He appeared to be five or six, but the Cranston's decided he was a newborn child. They created a birthdate for him. April 13. Not a Friday. On the fifth birthday of Joseph Cranston his biological mother hunted him down and took him home with her. Stolen. Lived a secret he kept even from himself.

Years after being abducted, Joseph studied to become a priest. He attended the Pittsburgh Theological Seminary. He hungered for that which was missing. He became a prolific reader. He read both inside and outside the boundaries of what was allowed. He sought out God in every sentence that he read. He searched for the word of God, the word that was not in the Bible. He rummaged through books that had been forbidden looking for that one word that would save him. He stared at graffiti, at billboards, at tattoos, hoping to see what was not meant to be known. But not a word of any of what Joseph read was true, or even approached the truth. Vulnerable and exhausted, he came to believe that he lived in a world empty of God. He cut his wrists; he bled. He drank water and cured his thirst. He was hungry, he ate. He touched the flesh of others to prove that something existed outside of him. Joseph needed someone to pour himself into, but he never found such a person, so he waited in the shadows. Hope and wait. God demands nothing more.

After he graduated and became a priest, he knocked on the doors of lonely women. He offered his own flesh and touch to replace the body and blood of Christ. He told these women that true forgiveness could not be experienced through words. He told them they had to suffer their way to this understanding of forgiveness. He explained to them that this was a lonely road, but he would guide them. He looked down upon these women and their innocent need to believe in sacred vows, their misplaced faith in living honest and pure lives, their obstinate refusal to covet or steal or murder. These women bored him. Day after day they came to him. Saturdays they came to the confessional. He forced them to doubt. He rested his hand on their hands and told them true all believers doubted. He rested his hand on their thigh and comforted them and told them faith without doubt is death. He told them he doubted God. Doubted the teachings of God. Doubted the body and blood of Christ. He cut his wrists while they watched with curiosity and awe. Blood will tell, he said. He made childish pinky promises with them. They looked into his eyes, a sea of wonder, uncertainty, and longing. He began seeking out women who were mad for sex, women who thought sex was the only way to redemption. He wanted little more than to become a prisoner of what he did to them. In the end, a man is all that he has done to other people. That is all that he is. Nothing more. A man is not an abstract being. He is an accumulation of everything he has ever done to any person who has come into his life. That is who a man truly is.

Until the morning of the fire. The morning of the fire, Father Joseph sat on the porch of the rectory staring, listening to the roaring sounds of the fire drown out the wails of his parishioners. One woman rushed over to Father Joseph and said, "It's God. It's God. He is the fire." He smiled at her and told her, "Yes, God is here with us. He is in everything we do to each other." He pointed to an oak tree that should have been burning. "God is inside that tree. He is that tree. Believe in that." He rose from his rocking chair, blessed the woman, then walked toward the steps of the burning church. He wanted to walk into the fire, to walk through the flames and come out on the other side. He was not so foolish as to think that the flames would cleanse him, and he did not think he would emerge from the flames unharmed. He assumed he would die by the fire. But he did believe that there was something that his burning flesh could reveal to him a moment before his death. A baptism of fire. His tongue burning. Angry voices mixing with joyful voices came from the fire. A serenade. As he neared the entrance to the burning church, the flames began licking at his skin, burning into his doubt. A firefighter rushed over to Father Joseph, grabbed him and pulled him away from the blazing fire and said: "Nothing can be saved, Father. Nothing. Nothing remains. Ashes."

Dazed, Father Joseph turned to the firefighter and whispered, "For we have brought nothing into the world, so we cannot take anything out if it either."

"Father?"

"Timothy. It is from Timothy." He looked at the darkened face of the firefighter. "The Bible. Nothing from nothing. To return as naked from the world as we were when he entered the world."

"Are you okay?" The firefighter asked. He looked around the street, searching for a doctor. "Should I find someone to help you?"

"No. No. Go back to your fight, and I will return to my struggle," Father Joseph replied. "Nothing good dwells in a man who does not surrender his body to be burned," he whispered to himself.

"Father?"

"Return to your work, son. There is too much heat here for me." He sat back down on the steps of the rectory. The firefighter returned to his battle. Father Joseph stared at the fires falling from the heavens and rising from hell and at the fires rising to the heavens and burning into hell. He felt the flames on his own skin. He rubbed his thumb into the palm of his hand, believing that the past could be erased, hoping that forgiveness was still possible. To be stripped of every happiness. The hour between dog and wolf. He became his own shadow and stared down into those creases in the palms of his hands, lilacs blooming and mud roads.

Hardy310

I want to use
the oxygen Destroyer.

Hardy310

Hardy310

NOT ONLY WAS HE DEAD, BUT HE FELT BAD, TOO

Eckhard Gerdes

Not only was he dead, but he felt bad, too. That's what I was thinking after that damned Salamander interrupted my reverie by shouting, "You killed him, and what's worse, you lied!" Oh, the Salamander? I'll explain that in a little bit. It gets a bit complicated, so stop me if I lose you. Let me know. I can go back over it again.

No, I never killed him. I never killed anyone. However, I have been accused of some weird shit in my time, but no one ever accused me of the shit he accused me of. It was bizarre. I was, according to him, secretly working in cahoots with the CIA, the NSA, the FBI, and Homeland Security to conspire against him and keep tabs on him because the government secretly knew how dangerous he was. I just walked away at that point. I have no idea what happened to him. I tried to care, but that was too hard. I am sorry. That is a place I cannot go back to.

He had a few problems, of course, but who doesn't? That really wasn't the issue. Everything had gone to ruin. I'd lost my job, lost my housing, was adrift on the far side of the continent without an anchor, and the life I had tried to stitch together just unraveled. No one, really, is to blame. It just couldn't be blended together like chum for fish.

You think the Salamander killed him? That's possible, I guess, but I don't think so, and here's why. He just accused me of killing him. If I'd killed him, then he'd know *he* hadn't killed him, but he wouldn't let on so readily. He'd pretend not to know. If he was *claiming* to know, then he actually *didn't* and was just bluffing. That meant that very likely *he* had killed him.

I think I'd worked that out. Okay, so how was I going to catch the Salamander? That was going to be a problem. Anytime a subject kills an object, consequences follow. I had to invent a device that would help me not only ward off those consequences, but also lead me into much safer territory.

The Salamander was one slippery fellow.

Maybe *I* am the Salamander. I am not sure. I have not looked into a mirror for a long while, but I do feel like I have had my tail torn off repeatedly throughout my life. Of course, as a Salamander, I can grow a new one.

"No, *I* am the Salamander!" comes the reply from some Kirk Douglas lookalike. Of course he's wrong, not because he looks like Kirk Douglas, but because he has no panache, which Douglas had plenty of.

Are you leading up to a discussion about Kirk Douglas's purchase of the screen rights to One Flew over the Cuckoo's Nest, *which he later transferred to his son Michael.*

Well, don't have to anymore. Thanks.

Actually, I feel like I have been away for a while. I have had to deal with my work obligations, and they are tough. I am teaching seven classes this semester, and that is actually a relatively low quantity for adjunct faculty. I have had colleagues who have taught more than a dozen at a time, out of necessity, of course.

Oh, and just when I was starting to think I was making sense. I lost my train of thought. It was coming through the station, and I swear I only closed my eyes for a minute, and when I came to, well, my train was long gone. I had to wait.

But I drew the line at splitting a Chateaubriand-for-two between three people. I'd let them have two, split three ways, so that each would have two-thirds of a Chateaubriand. That seemed like a good number.

If you don't like that one, let us know. We can swap it for another.

We have an employee whose entire job is to run numbers.

Line up, youse guys. Toe the line! On the count of three! One, two, GO!

Okay, maybe not *that* guy.

I am just happy to be here. I actually have two days of free time. I cannot believe it. As an adjunct instructor, I have to teach twice as many classes as a full-time instructor just to make half the money. But the systems is what's horrid. Everyone knows that. "HEY, WHERE ARE YOU GOING WITH THAT SOAP BOX? I WAS JUST GOING TO SAY SOME thing..............."

Ooh, an extra-long ellipsis? Ahhhhhh! Prescriptive grammaticians everywhere have fainted, right? No, I don't think so.

Pan the door. Uh, oh, you opened that? Okay, we'll deal with it.

Why "pan"? Well, what else would you do to a door? The Doors were gold for Elektra Records. If they were gold, then "panning" would be an appropriate verb.

Okay, glad we've got that solved.

But when I was served my meal, and the glass bell lid was pulled off the platter, suddenly something happened.

I sneezed.

I wheezed.

I pleased whomever I could when I would.

I was ready to repeat that, but then the air changed. It was realized to me that I should keep my cards close. Someone might be looking over my shoulder. Good thing I have another one.

THE MAN WHO TIED HIS SHOES AND THE WOMAN WHO FED IMAGINARY PIGEONS

Jason E. Rolfe

"There's an idea that hell is other people. My idea is that it might be repetition."— Stephen King

Monday

Daniil Ivanovich Yuvachev caught the metro at Mayakovskaya station. Although he lived between Mayakovskaya and Chernishevskaya (a nice, quiet, and very residential neighbourhood known for its fresh food market and pre-revolutionary architecture) he spent the majority of his day at work on Nevsky Prospekt. His office, adjacent to the Mertens Trade Centre, was a short ride to and a brief walk from, the Nevsky Prospekt metro station. Daniil Yuvachev often spent the brief journey writing in his notebook. Although Daniil earned his living writing reports, he considered himself, first and foremost, a poet and a playwright. When he wasn't writing in his notebook, Daniil Ivanovich watched those around him. Take Monday for example. Daniil Ivanovich spent the entire trip, from Mayakovskaya station to Nevsky Prospekt, watching a man tie, untie, and then retie his shoelaces. First the man untied his shoelace. He then read the newspaper. While turning pages the man seemed to notice for the first time that his shoelace was untied and bent down to retie it. Having tied it, he untied the other shoelace and went back to reading his newspaper. While turning pages the man seemed to notice for the first time that his other shoelace was untied and bent down to retie that one. Having tied it, he untied the other shoelace and went back to reading his newspaper. Daniil Ivanovich faithfully recorded the man's odd behaviour in his notebook, unsure how, when or if he would employ it in his writing.

Nothing unusual happened during his walk from the metro station to his office building which was, as previously mentioned, adjacent to the Mertens Trade Centre on Nevsky Prospekt. The unusual never occurred during Daniil Ivanovich's walk from the metro station to work. Using Monday as our example, Daniil Ivanovich walked from the Nevsky Prospekt metro station to work, passing Kazan Cathedral and the Singer building as usual. As per the norm he passed an old woman feeding imaginary pigeons. When the bread was gone, the old woman crumpled the plain brown paper bag and threw it on the ground. The bread and the empty bag remained untouched until an elderly gentleman happened by with a broom. He swept the bread up and placed it back in the plain brown paper bag before returning it to the old woman. As Daniil Ivanovich passed the old woman, she began feeding the imaginary pigeons again. Curious, he turned and watched her toss the bread to the imagined birds until she had once again emptied the bag. Once the plain brown paper bag was empty she crumpled it up and tossed it on the ground. Both the bread and the empty bag remained where they fell until a second elderly man happened by with a broom. He swept the bread up, returned it to the plain brown paper bag, and then returned the plain brown paper bag to the old woman who, without further delay, began feeding the imaginary pigeons. Daniil Ivanovich noted the old woman's odd behaviour in his notebook and continued his commute to work.

When Daniil Ivanovich arrived at work he greeted the new receptionist with a warm smile. "First day?" he said. The new receptionist snapped her bubble gum. Otherwise, she ignored him completely. "Are you enjoying things so far?" Daniil Ivanovich asked. The new receptionist blew a bubble and then sucked it back into her mouth. She neither spoke nor offered him a passing glance. "How are you getting along?" Daniil Ivanovich asked again, to which she responded by snapping her bubble gum.

There was an awkward pause.

"Well," Daniil Ivanovich said. "I suppose I should get to work."

The receptionist blew another bubble, but this time the bubble fell from her mouth. It landed on Daniil Ivanovich's arm. Without a word the receptionist, whose name he could not remember, reached for her purse and promptly removed an open pack of gum. Daniil noted that the pack was exactly one piece short of full. The receptionist took a second piece and popped it in her mouth. At no point did she acknowledge Daniil's presence.

There was yet another awkward pause, after which Daniil went into his office and closed the door.

Daniil Ivanovich's primary role with The Company involved the writing, filing, and shredding of reports. He was greeted each and every morning by the same list of forty-two required reports. He spent the first three hours of his day writing them, the next three filing them. Between the fourth and fifth hours he took a brief lunch and, as discussed in another story, stared out the office window while his mind wandered along Nevsky Prospekt. When his mind returned from its brief jaunts, Daniil Ivanovich attended the Old Man's meeting. The reports were never discussed. The Old Man preached the need for a passionate, enthusiastic workforce willing to surrender its life to The Company and its glorious ideals. He said these things in such a way that each and every employee understood them as unquestionable commands rather than encouraging prosaicisms. After the meeting, Daniil Ivanovich finished filing the forty-two reports, and then spent the final three hours of his day shredding them (for reasons known only to the Old Man).

Once he had completed the task of shredding the reports he'd written, Daniil Ivanovich left the office. He passed the receptionist on his way out. "Another day, another dollar," he said. The receptionist, who had only started with The Company that morning, snapped her bubble gum. Otherwise, she ignored him completely. "Well, have a nice evening," Daniil Ivanovich said. The receptionist blew a bubble and then sucked it back into her mouth. She neither spoke nor offered him a passing glance. "I'll see you tomorrow morning!" Daniil Ivanovich said, to which she responded by snapping her bubble gum.

There was an awkward pause after which Daniil left work for the night.

Tuesday

The following morning Daniil Ivanovich Yuvachev caught the metro at Mayakovskaya station. Although he lived between Mayakovskaya and Chernishevskaya (a nice, quiet, and very residential neighbourhood known for its fresh food market and pre-revolutionary architecture) he spent the majority of his day at work on Nevsky Prospekt. His office, adjacent to the Mertens Trade Centre, was a short ride to and a brief walk from, the Nevsky Prospekt metro station. Daniil Yuvachev often spent the brief journey writing in his notebook. Although Daniil earned his living writing reports, he considered himself, first and foremost, a poet and a playwright. When he wasn't writing in his notebook, Daniil Ivanovich watched those around him. Take Tuesday for example. Daniil Ivanovich spent the entire trip, from Mayakovskaya station to Nevsky Prospekt, watching a man tie, untie, and then retie his shoelaces. First the man untied his shoelace. He then read the newspaper. While turning pages the man seemed to notice for the first time that his shoelace was untied and bent down to retie it. Having tied it, he untied the other shoelace and went back to reading his newspaper. While turning pages the man seemed to notice for the first time that his other shoelace was untied and bent down to retie that one. Having tied it, he untied the other shoelace and went back to reading his newspaper. Daniil Ivanovich faithfully recorded the man's odd behaviour in his notebook, unsure how, when or if he would employ it in his writing.

Nothing unusual happened during his walk from the metro station to his office building which was, as previously mentioned, adjacent to the Mertens Trade Centre on Nevsky Prospekt. The unusual never occurred during Daniil Ivanovich's walk from the metro station to work. Using Tuesday as our example, Daniil Ivanovich walked from the Nevsky Prospekt metro station to work, passing Kazan Cathedral and the Singer building as usual. As per the norm he passed an old woman feeding imaginary pigeons. When the bread was gone, the old woman crumpled the plain brown paper bag and threw it on the ground. The bread and the empty bag remained untouched until an elderly gentleman happened by with a broom. He swept the bread up and placed it back in the plain brown paper bag before returning it to the old woman. As Daniil Ivanovich passed the old woman, she began feeding the imaginary pigeons again. Curious, he turned and watched her toss the bread to the imagined birds until she had once again emptied the bag. Once the plain brown paper bag was empty she crumpled it up and tossed it on the ground. Both the bread and the empty bag remained where they fell until a second elderly man happened by with a broom. He swept the bread up, returned it to the plain brown paper bag, and then returned the plain brown paper bag to the old woman who, without further delay, began feeding the imaginary pigeons. Daniil Ivanovich noted the old woman's odd behaviour in his notebook and continued his commute to work. He thought about the repetitiveness of their lives. The man who tied and untied his shoes every day and the woman who fed the same imaginary pigeons from the same crumpled brown paper bag seemed completely oblivious to the clockwork dreariness of their lives.

When Daniil Ivanovich arrived at work he greeted the new receptionist with a warm smile. "Another day," he said. The receptionist, who had only started with The Company the day before, snapped her bubble gum. Otherwise, she ignored him completely. "Here we are again," Daniil Ivanovich said. The receptionist blew a bubble and then sucked it back into her mouth. She neither spoke nor offered him a passing glance. "How are you getting along so far?" Daniil Ivanovich asked, to which she responded by snapping her bubble gum.

There was an awkward pause.

"Well," Daniil Ivanovich said. "I suppose I should get to work."

The receptionist blew another bubble, but this time the bubble fell from her mouth. It landed atop the other bubble on Daniil Ivanovich's arm. Without a word the receptionist, whose name he could not remember, reached for her purse and removed an open pack of gum. Daniil noted that the pack was exactly two pieces short of full. The receptionist removed a third piece and popped it in her mouth. At no point did she acknowledge Daniil's presence.

There was yet another awkward pause, after which Daniil went into his office and closed the door.

Daniil Ivanovich's primary role with The Company involved the writing, filing, and shredding of reports. He was greeted each and every morning by the same list of forty-two required reports. He spent the first three hours of his day writing them, the next three filing them. Between the fourth and fifth hours he took a brief lunch and, as discussed in another story, stared out the office window while his mind wandered along Nevsky Prospekt. When his mind returned from its brief jaunts, Daniil Ivanovich attended the Old Man's meeting. The reports were never discussed. The Old Man preached the need for a passionate, enthusiastic workforce willing to surrender its life to The Company and its glorious ideals. He said these things in such a way that each and every employee understood them as unquestionable commands rather than encouraging prosaicisms. After the meeting, Daniil Ivanovich finished filing the forty-two reports, and then spent the final three hours of his day shredding them (for reasons known only to the Old Man).

Once he had completed the task of shredding the reports he'd written, Daniil Ivanovich left the office. He passed the receptionist on his way out. "Another day, another dollar," he said. The receptionist, who had only started with The Company the day before, snapped her bubble gum. Otherwise, she ignored him completely. "Well, have a nice evening," Daniil Ivanovich said. The receptionist blew a bubble and then sucked it back into her mouth. She neither spoke nor offered him a passing glance. "I'll see you tomorrow morning!" Daniil Ivanovich said, to which she responded by snapping her bubble gum.

There was an awkward pause after which Daniil left work for the night.

Wednesday (and every day thereafter)

The next morning Daniil Ivanovich Yuvachev caught the metro at Mayakovskaya station. Although he lived between Mayakovskaya and Chernishevskaya (a nice, quiet, and very residential neighbourhood known for its fresh food market and pre-revolutionary architecture) he spent the majority of his day at work on Nevsky Prospekt. His office, adjacent to the Mertens Trade Centre, was a short ride to and a brief walk from, the Nevsky Prospekt metro station. Daniil Yuvachev often spent the brief journey writing in his notebook. Although Daniil earned his living writing reports, he considered himself, first and foremost, a poet and a playwright. When he wasn't writing in his notebook, Daniil Ivanovich watched those around him. Take Wednesday for example. Daniil Ivanovich spent the entire trip, from Mayakovskaya station to Nevsky Prospekt, watching a man tie, untie, and then retie his shoelaces. First the man untied his shoelace. He then read the newspaper. While turning pages the man seemed to notice for the first time that his shoelace was untied and bent down to retie it.

Having tied it, he untied the other shoelace and went back to reading his newspaper. While turning pages the man seemed to notice for the first time that his other shoelace was untied and bent down to retie that one. Having tied it, he untied the other shoelace and went back to reading his newspaper. Daniil Ivanovich faithfully recorded the man's odd behaviour in his notebook, unsure how, when or if he would employ it in his writing.

Nothing unusual happened during his walk from the metro station to his office building which was, as previously mentioned, adjacent to the Mertens Trade Centre on Nevsky Prospekt. The unusual never occurred during Daniil Ivanovich's walk from the metro station to work. Using Wednesday as our example, Daniil Ivanovich walked from the Nevsky Prospekt metro station to work, passing Kazan Cathedral and the Singer building as usual. As per the norm he passed an old woman feeding imaginary pigeons. When the bread was gone, the old woman crumpled the plain brown paper bag and threw it on the ground. The bread and the empty bag remained untouched until an elderly gentleman happened by with a broom. He swept the bread up and placed it back in the plain brown paper bag before returning it to the old woman. As Daniil Ivanovich passed the old woman, she began feeding the imaginary pigeons again. Curious, he turned and watched her toss the bread to the imagined birds until she had once again emptied the bag. Once the plain brown paper bag was empty she crumpled it up and tossed it on the ground. Both the bread and the empty bag remained where they fell until a second elderly man happened by with a broom. He swept the bread up, returned it to the plain brown paper bag, and then returned the plain brown paper bag to the old woman who, without further delay, began feeding the imaginary pigeons. Daniil Ivanovich noted the old woman's odd behaviour in his notebook and continued his commute to work.

When Daniil Ivanovich arrived at work he greeted the new receptionist with a warm smile. "Another day," he said. The receptionist, who had only started with The Company two days earlier, snapped her bubble gum. Otherwise, she ignored him completely. "Here we are again," Daniil Ivanovich said. The receptionist blew a bubble and then sucked it back into her mouth. She neither spoke nor offered him a passing glance. "How are you getting along so far?" Daniil Ivanovich asked, to which she responded by snapping her bubble gum.

There was an awkward pause.

"Well," Daniil Ivanovich said. "I suppose I should get to work."

The receptionist blew another bubble, but this time the bubble fell from her mouth. It landed atop two other bubbles on Daniil Ivanovich's arm. Without a word the receptionist, whose name he could not remember, reached for her purse and removed an open pack of gum. Daniil noted that the pack was exactly three pieces short of full. The receptionist removed a fourth piece and popped it in her mouth. At no point did she acknowledge Daniil's presence.

There was yet another awkward pause, after which Daniil went into his office and closed the door. Before getting down to work he thought about the man and the old woman he encountered each and every day on his way to work. He thought about the repetitiveness of their lives. The man who tied and untied his shoes every day and the woman who fed the same imaginary pigeons from the same crumpled brown paper bag seemed completely oblivious to the clockwork dreariness of their lives. He pitied them.

Infinitum

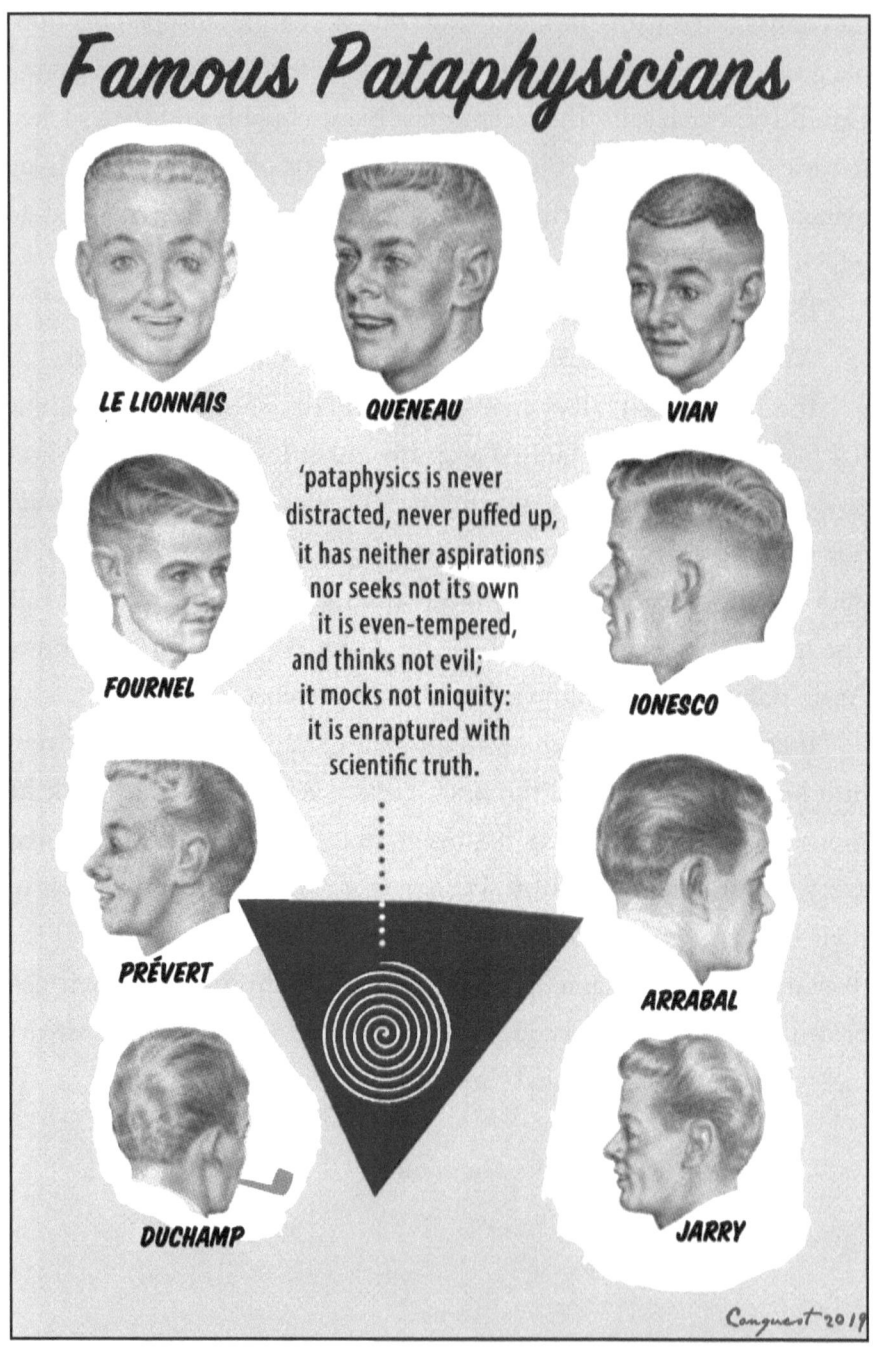

Norman Conquest

TROUSER HERMITS

Rhys Hughes

L ooking at footage of the pedestrians in a European city at the beginning of the 20th Century, it struck me, as it generally strikes most modern people, not that I am quite as modern as I should be, how many of the men back then wore hats as a normal part of their everyday attire. Women too, of course, but women often still wear hats. The hat hasn't really gone away as far as the female head is concerned. But among men it is no longer common. While studying this footage I was told by another observer that in those days, "Men would never go out without a hat," and everything I saw on the screen seemed to confirm this judgment.

But then it occurred to me that such an ubiquitous expectation contained seeds of doom for certain unlucky souls. A man might have possessed only one hat. It is vital that he goes out. He looks for the hat but can't find it. Maybe it has decayed overnight into dust. Perhaps the cat ran off with it. Possibly it is simply lost without explanation in the manner of so many other domestic objects. The hat has gone. There is no spare hat and so the man is stuck indoors. Men never go out without a hat, and he has none, therefore it is impossible for him to go out.

But he must go out, it is important, maybe his daughter needs rescuing from a cad or he has to invent the electric brougham. What are the options? Well, to improvise a hat is the obvious solution. A tea cosy makes an excellent item of headgear. I know this from experience. So do many others. I believe that it was Stewart Lee who once said something along the lines of, "Put a man in a room with nothing but a tea cosy and if within the hour he isn't wearing it on his head, then he is the very definition of a boring person." I concur wholeheartedly and wholeheadedly with this sentiment.

The tea cosy hat is superior to a topper.

The main reason I first tried wearing one was to spoof Aleister Crowley, that half fraudulent, half brilliant, half ludicrous magus, and if those fractions don't add up it's entirely apt, because the parts of his life didn't add up either. He liked to wear strange, soft, comfy looking things on his head. They weren't really hats as such, more like an unholy conjunction of turban, cushion and mitre. Almost exactly like tea cosies in fact! I wore the tea cosy and spoofed him and it was a satisfying experience. Had I been born one hundred years earlier than I was, I could have gone out wearing it and made my way to the nearest hat shop in order to purchase a proper hat. The tea cosy might look absurd but at least it can pass as a type of hat, and that would be enough to permit me to walk the streets without censure.

Or rather, there would be censure in the form of ridicule, for a man in a tea cosy is a natural target of fun, but no censure in the form of social outrage. And the moment I reached the hat shop I would be safe, safe to buy a proper hat and emerge like a true man, a man able to hold his head up high in public, not just in order to keep the new hat balanced on top, but because I would have nothing to fear. The tea cosy could be stuffed into one of the pockets of my trousers. No one need know it was there. If the bulge showed too prominently, people would merely assume I had been walking in a street where prostitutes gathered but without engaging their services. No shame and no worries. I would be a man of my time again.

Trouser pockets, however, are a subject that brings me to another consideration of greater relevance to our own society. If you own a hat in the modern age and your cat runs off with it, what difficulties do you face? Very few compared with your ancestor of a century ago. But imagine you only possess one pair of trousers and these trousers suddenly disappear overnight! Now you are in trouble irrespective of the year of your birth. Even if the trousers don't completely disappear, even if they only tear and flap open at the crotch, the result is the same. You will be unable to visit the trouser shop for another pair of trousers. To visit that shop requires you to walk there and to walk to a shop, even a trouser shop, necessitates that you are already wearing trousers. A man without cheese might plausibly go to a cheesemonger's but no man goes to the vendor of trousers in the nude. The scenarios belong to separate categories. A man with only one pair of trousers who loses the use of those trousers is stuck indoors for the remainder of his days. He is a prisoner.

But maybe it is kinder to refer to him as a hermit? There are no political, criminal or moral millstones around the neck of a hermit, as there are around a criminal's neck. A hermit retires from society. We walk down the street and we see curtains twitch in the windows of the houses we pass. Shadowy faces behind them. There are tens of thousands of trouser hermits in the cities of our civilisation, men trapped into a life of enclosure by massive trouser trauma. They could be rescued easily enough. A pair of new trousers fed through the letter flap of each unhappy abode. But we are ignorant of them, their desperate need. We pass on, oblivious, striding in our own good trousers. Also we are wise, we are prudent, we are prepared. At home we have many trousers, we aren't as feckless as these lost trapped souls in the rooms of those houses who are destined to dine frugally on what little food remains in their cupboards before going on to devour cobwebs, furniture and grime.

The circle can be completed, even though it's not really a circle but just a lump of an unspecified kind. The trouser hermit has no wife or family to come to the rescue and his work colleagues simply don't care enough about him to seek him out. Yes, he can attempt to improvise trousers by knotting together towels and dishcloths, but he is too clumsy to do so. He cannot call for help on the telephone because the telephone was one of the first things he ate when the tinned food ran out. He is too shy to bang on the window at passersby for help. He is the perfect anchorite, stuck to the seabed of his own reticence even though the vessel of normal life has broken free and gone sailing off without him. What can he do? He will lurk because lurking is one of his natural skills. And at the base of some little-used wardrobe in the spare room he kept for guests who never came, he will find items of old clothing he had forgotten about. Our final view of him, in our hungry mind's eye, shows him squatting in this gloomy space munching on hats, the hats of a former time, the hats that are no longer crucial for a fulfilled life, the hats of sundry sizes and miscellaneous materials that betrayed the scalps of our elders with historic itchings.

LEAVING THE FARM
Peter Cherches & Norman Conquest

The Farmer's Daughter lies in bed, dreaming of city and sin. I'm sick and tired of this Farmer's Daughter shit, she tells herself. I'm just the butt end of a flood of crappy jokes, she thinks. She dreams of running away, to a place where she can be lost in the crowd, be herself, no longer the "Farmer's Daughter" of laughter and derision.

The following morning, weary from a night of insomniac nocturnal daydreaming, she decides to take the bull by the horns and make her getaway. She rushes off to the one-lane dirt road, the town's main thoroughfare, with nothing but a small travel bag and the clothes on her back, and flags down the bus.

She sits in the back, far from the three strange men in suits, each seated alone, with fluorescent skin and foam oozing from the corners of their mouths, the only other passengers. From time to time they turn around to stare at her. One of the men, a traveling salesman, brushes and encyclopedias, a one-two punch, chats with the driver, whose eyes are glued to the rearview mirror. The Farmer's Daughter can hear snippets of the conversation. They are talking about fishing, and the salesman must be quite a good fisherman since the driver keeps saying things like, "Wow! That's something! Really?" After a while the salesman runs out of fish tales, turns to sit sideways—an unnatural position—and leers at the Farmer's Daughter. She squirms, glances down at her lap, then begins rummaging through her bag, searching for nothing, just avoiding his ogle. She looks up, catches his eye briefly, and thinks: This man looks *very* familiar. She averts her eyes again, as she knows if she acknowledges him he'll strike up a conversation, and conversation inevitably leads to calamity. She closes her eyes, leans back in her seat and pretends to nap. She imagines the view outside her window, the endless string of farms, a cinematic blur to her mind's eye.

When the bus reaches Los Angeles she steps into the station's waiting room. It's hot and musty. The ceiling fans are out of service, and it's the dead of summer. The benches are occupied by elderly men and women, immigrants, the Farmer's Daughter thinks. They're seated upright as if at a church service, some wearing their Sunday best, tattered yet dignified. A few hold swizzle stick-sized American flags and wear expectant expressions, but most look as though they've lost their faith. She wonders if they are coming or going.

The Farmer's Daughter leans against a wall. She opens her travel bag to fish out her compact and out jumps an iguana. How this iguana got in her bag she does not know, but it's a particularly aggressive reptile, and it jumps on the Farmer's Daughter, taking her unawares and knocking her to the floor as it begins to rip off her clothes. She screams, but nobody comes over to her aid. The Farmer's Daughter's dress is in tatters, skin exposed, as the iguana runs roughshod over her body, scratching and biting until she's a bloody mess.

Lying on the floor, wounded, bleeding, exhausted, defeated, she hears an announcement: the bus has arrived. The elderly immigrants rise from their benches and proceed, single-file, expressionless, to the exit.

The Farmer's Daughter looks up and sees a flashing neon sign she had not noticed before.

"Today is the first day of the rest of your life."

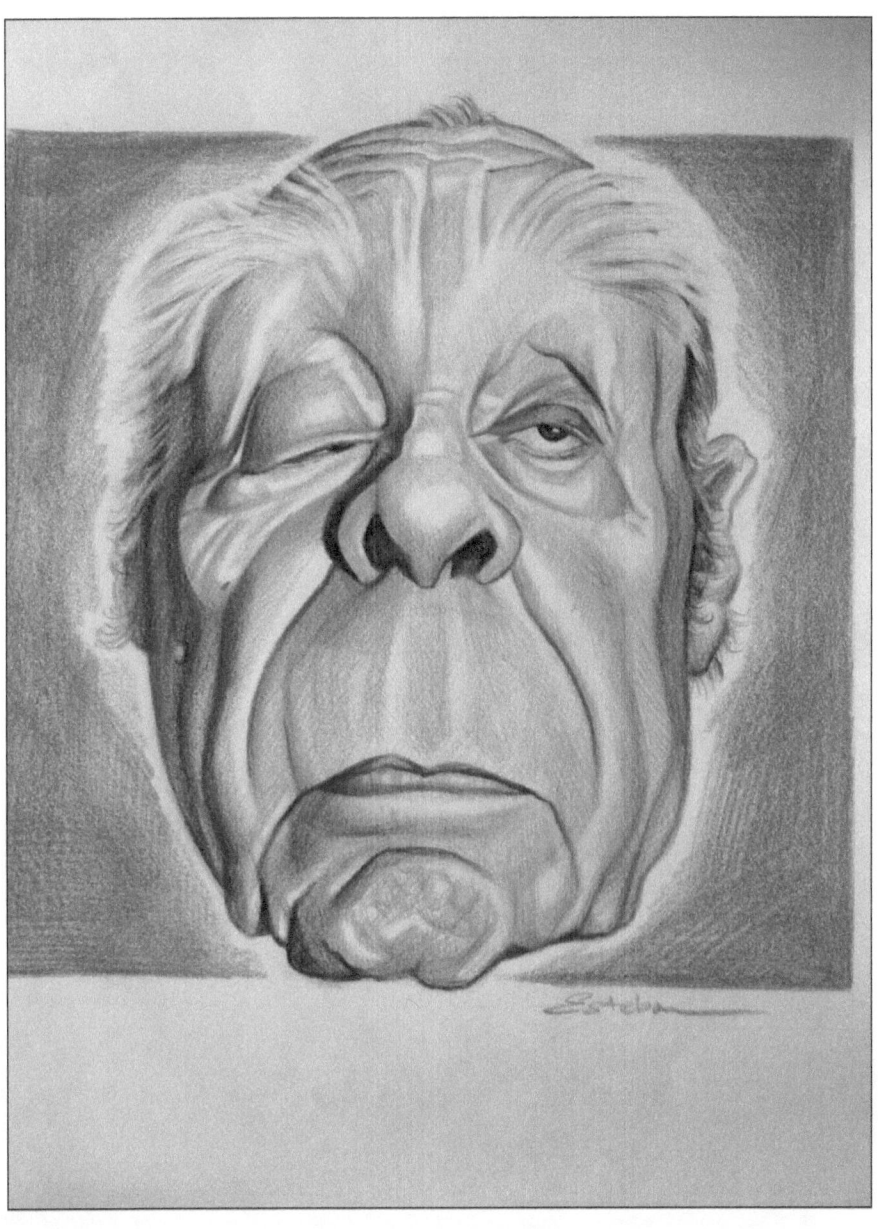

Esteban Isnardi

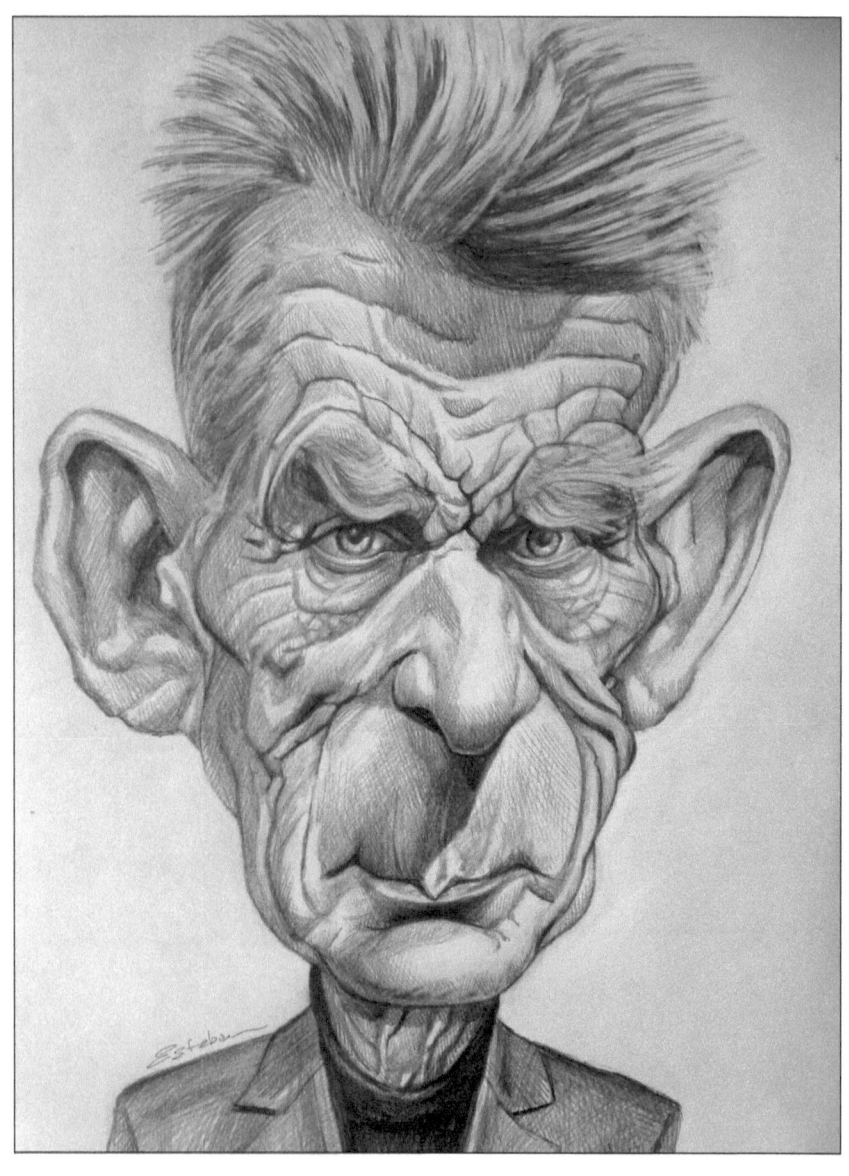

Esteban Isnardi

BECKETT'S BAR

Mark Axelrod

O f all the unusual investments made by artists, this one might be the most unusual. Not because of it being a restaurant, but for the circumstances surrounding its creation. It all started in the late 80's when an impecunious novice writer by the name of M.R. Axelrod had an opportunity to meet Beckett. The reason for that meeting was because Axelrod had met the son-in-law of one Brian Coffey while Axelrod was on a Fulbright to study at Oxford. During a conversation between Axelrod and Coffey's son-in-law Beckett's name came up. At the time, Axelrod didn't know the son-in-law was Coffey's son-in-law nor did he know he was a close friend of Beckett's, but the former suggested that Axelrod contact his father-in-law about the possibility of meeting Beckett in the future.

Flash forward several years when Axelrod, still an impecunious novice writer, was awarded a residency at the Camargo Foundation in Cassis, France. Prior to leaving for the South of France, Axelrod wrote the maestro about an interview in Paris. Beckett wrote back, "For an interview, no; for a chat, by all means." It was done. During a break from the residency, Axelrod journeyed to Paris to meet Beckett at the café inside the Hôtel Saint Jacques, on the Rue Des Ecoles. It so happened, that on the same day, Axelrod had picked up a copy of an English periodical called *Passion*, the cover of which read: "*Les 100 Poids Lourds Des Lettres*" with a picture of a certain Regine Deforges on the cover. The blurb beneath the title read ""Un *hit-parade* des 100 per-sonnes-editeurs, écrivains, et...poètes-qui constituent le Tout-Paris des lettres." What Axelrod found odd, was that Beckett wasn't included so, among other things Axelrod talked to Beckett about, he mentioned the article. Beckett was toying with his reading glasses when he said, "I forgive them." Axelrod really didn't.

When Axelrod returned to the United States, he contacted Coffey and mentioned the periodical and the egregious omission of Beckett. He thought something should be done about it and Coffey agreed. Axelrod thought Beckett should do something to "solidify his legacy" and suggested he open a restaurant. Beckett really didn't care about his legacy, but Axelrod convinced the *maestro* that if nothing else it would remind all those people in Paris who didn't think he was a heavyweight that, in fact, he was. And if not a heavyweight, then a gourmand.

Encouraged by both Axelrod and Coffey, Beckett looked for a location to open the restaurant and found it at, where else, at 8 Rue Godot de Mauroy. The restaurant was set to open at Christmas, 1989, but, alas, Beckett died shortly before it opened. The original chef, a former student of Bocuse, was so distraught about the death he couldn't continue and a new chef, Horacio Oliveira, from Buenos Aires, took over. Axelrod would have recommended the Saint Jacques Crue dur sa Coquille (which was one of Beckett's favorites) had the bar continued; alas, the bar has gone out of business, out of business the bar has gone, gone, as in no longer in business, out of the business, the business out. What remains is that Axelrod remains an impecunious novice writer. An impecunious and novice writer he. Alas. Here, the last menu. I can't go eat. I'll eat.

CLOSING CREDITS
IN
THE CULTURE WARS

Charles Holdefer

Take One:

Postmodernists in Love

"Darling, I can't fight it anymore."

She swallowed deeply.

"Truly, I feel so much…" She lifted her fingers and scratched quotation marks into the air: "'*love.*'"

His breaths came faster.

"Oh, baby, are you sure that's what you…" He lifted his fingers and scratched back: "'*mean?*'"

She nodded and they reached out, their fingers entwined as they gazed into each other's eyes, speechless.

Take Two:

Constitutional Originalists in Love

"Honey, darn it anyway, there's something that's got to be said."

He drew up his shoulders.

"What?" she asked. "Go ahead. And I don't care if it's not politically correct. Shoot!"

"I love you. Hear me? That's the straight talk and I stand my ground. And now I'm going to kiss you."

She leaned toward him.

"Yes, do! Our founding fathers were great kissers."

Take Three:

Woke Folk in Love

"Do you have something to tell me?" she asked.

He smiled as he rubbed her back. "Actually, I do."

"No, wait. Let me guess."

"Sure," he said, reaching for more oil. "I'm right here. I'm listening."

"You love me, don't you? Without preconceptions or non-reciprocal expectations. That's it, right?"

He sighed. "I couldn't have put it better myself."

Take Four:

Dudes in Love

"Babe, something's gotta be said."

"Wait," she told him. "First turn your cap backwards. Will you do that for me? It makes you so handsome."

He reached up and gripped the bill and readjusted it. She pressed her hands together and cooed.

"Here it is," he said. "I frickin' I love you."

"Oh, awesome!"

"I can't take my eyes off you."

She looked down at her shirt. "You like them?"

Take Five:

Nation Builders in Love

"Listen up, sweetie. Got something to say. But don't take it wrong." He sighed. "Sometimes I'm misunderstood."

"*¿Qué?*"

"It's like this. I love you, see?"

"*¡Qué!*"

"But I need to tie you up when we do it."

"*¿Por qué?*"

"That's how I like it. The way I express myself is manifest and cannot be abridged. Now give me your wrists."

LIMB

Catherine D'Avis

t was Guy Carrell who taught me to have compassion for all living things.

He said, *Fill your heart with love for all things, Laurine. Even fat-flies, even dirt-worms. Even those you want to hate.*

I'm sending compassion to a spirit-mite as it throws itself against the window. It buzzes with fury, crazed with a desire to live, to be out in the wide blue. I balance on the stair rail and send it calming vibrations. I am close enough to see the fine hairs on its body.

"Relax. I will free you, *mon petit.*"

I stretch my body and reach up. I'm glad to have grown so tall this last year. The spirit-mite cries as though it will explode. It sobs and wails for life. I manage to push the window up a few inches. In the same movement, I drop from the rail and land with a thump on the stairs. I pick up my school bag.

"Laurine?" Maman is standing at her bedroom door. She blinks, still bleary with sleep, and pushes her hair from her eyes. She doesn't hold her dressing gown closed, exposing the center curves of her sun-tanned breasts. Below, her plump belly crisscrossed with white stretch marks. "Are you going to school already, *cherie*? It seems so early."

The rumble of a man's heavy sleep breathing travels from her bedroom and up the stairs. The new lover must have stayed the night. Through the door, I see an olive-toned foot, sticking out of the edge of the bed covers.

Maman steps out of the room and pulls the door closed behind her. "Oh, Laurine, he's wonderful." She means her new lover. She looks me up and down, taking in my school-clothes, the pleated skirt, the white blouse, the striped tie, the white socks pulled halfway to my knees. "Have a wonderful day, *ma cherie.*"

Her eyes shine in a way I haven't seen since Guy Carrell was here.

✳

Sunlight pours through the patio doors onto the kitchen table and the remains of the reckless meal Maman and her new lover ate last night. Pipis and toasted sea urchin, ginger smooth venus in sorrel and comfort sauce, wait-and-see pie and raw silversides in stargazer-paste, all reduced to so much dirty crockery. There are crumbs of home-baked ginger-seed cake everywhere and two crystal sour-berry wine glasses, one with red lip stain smeared around the edge. The ashtray is piled high with the ends of hash-flower sticks.

I recognize these greedy leftovers. Maman cooked a similar meal not so long ago for Guy Carrell.

✳

"You have to *blitz* them, Laurine," she'd said, as she loaded up the dishwasher. It was the morning after the first night Guy Carrell stayed and she had dark, happy circles under her eyes. *Blitz* was a term Maman used for a lot of things - sorting through cupboards, losing weight, selling real estate. She ran her hand over her forehead. Housework has always worn her out. "Hook them in! Food and sex are a man's weakest point and a woman's strongest weapon." She looked out the window and smiled a private smile.

Maman has other *blitz* tricks too, apart from cooking amazing food. I've seen her collection of silk-leaf undergarments, her white crystal stockings, the garter belts which pinch her thighs just so, her long sex boots and her silk succulent threads. I've heard her secret things, cried out in the small hours of the night.

There are some things I'm beginning to understand.

✳

The day of Guy Carrell's accident, I found Maman at the kitchen table with her head flopped down between her arms. I poured her a glass of water.

"I read the paper," she said. "I knew straight away it was him. *Mon dieu*, I can barely tell you what happened." She took a gulp of water. Her eyes were filled with drunken tears. She'd let her eye-makeup get messed up. I knew then it had to be something dreadful. "It was a mad woman in a pink, yes, *pink*, Seat Marbella who ran him over." It seemed to be the pinkness of the car which upset her more than anything. "They don't know if he'll make it. He's in intensive care. And no, before you say anything, I can't go and see him. Not after all that's happened. Not in a hospital. They are dreadful places. Promise me you'll never step inside a hospital."

But I've already made up my mind to visit him, whether she wants me to go or not.

✳

The first time we met Guy Carrell, he was hitch-hiking with a skateboard under one arm.

Maman stopped the car, "Où tu vas, *cheri?*"

He gazed at Maman without blinking and came home with us. He ate some of Maman's ginger cake with a little smoked cardamon krettle and stayed. He used to sing to Maman, in the evenings, when they sat on the porch swing with their legs intertwined. They drank sour-berry wine and scooped up pickled sea-elves with pieces of cake.

After Guy Carrell moved out, Maman took to eating jar after jar of marinated cockle hearts and canned sugar clams in marigold oil. I found her at the kitchen table late one night with the jars and the cans spread around her. The moon shone through the patio doors and the light made her cheekbones shine. Her eyes were bright in the half-dark.

I said, "Why don't you ask him to come back?"

She picked up a sugar-clam with her fingers and dropped it onto her tongue. The marigold oil ran down her chin. She said, "To a man, lust for a woman's body and greed for her food are all wrapped up in one. Food and sex, sex and food. If we all had as much love as we needed, then no one would be overweight." She sighed. She has always carried a few extra pounds. "In this world, a woman has to take all she can get. She must be ruthless. She must treat herself as she would a newborn baby because that's all she is, Laurine. She's a little baby in a hard, cold world."

❋

The hospital bed is surrounded by wires and tubes and beeping machines. I'm not even sure Guy Carrell knows I'm there, sitting by his side. The scrubbed-sterile antiseptic smell is everywhere. His face is bare without his blue make-up, one side of it so swollen he is almost unrecognizable. His expression is wiped clean.

His eyes open a crack. We sit in silence for a long time. Jittery footsteps echo in the corridors. In the distance someone moans with pain. Guy Carrell's breathing is raspy and uncertain. His hands are limp by his sides and covered in bandages. More time goes by. My eyes drift to the place in the bed where one of Guy Carrell's legs ought to be.

He whispers. "Some limbs can grow, Laurine. Some limbs can't. She'll never know what it's like to keep loving someone without end." I know he means Maman.

He closes his eyes. He's not going to say any more.

❋

There was one particular lazy day last summer. The details have stayed in my mind, the way the taste of a delicious meal can stay with you. Guy Carrell and I walked back up from the sands, swinging our arms. We were both an indulgent, golden brown. He pushed his wet hair back from his forehead. Blue kohl ran in streaks down his cheeks.

He paused to look back down the hill. "One day, I'll leave this island and I'll never come back."

"Never?" I said.

"Never."

※

I slip my hand under the cool hospital sheets. I find Guy Carrell's sleeping cock and grasp it until it stiffens, slightly at first, then completely. A burrowed animal waking up. Neither of us say a word. He never opens his eyes.

A spirit-mite buzzes in front of our faces. It wants to find a way outside. I pray it will make it, although I know there is barely a chance.

smells like teen pataphysics

Norman Conquest

A VERBO-VISUAL COLLECTION OF IMPOSSIBLE SOLUTIONS, PATAPHYSICAL EVIDENCE, SIGNS OF THE PHENOMENON, OSCILLATING PYRAMIDS, AND LUMINOUS VAPORS. THIS UNEXPURGATED EDITION IS ILLUSTRATED WITH UBU-DYSTOPIAN CHARTS, UNPUBLISHED DIAGRAMS, NEWLY DISCOVERED SCHEMATA, AND RARE ILLUMINATED PHOTOGRAPHS. ALSO INCLUDED ARE NORMAN CONQUEST'S GROUNDBREAKING PHILOSOPHICAL EXPERIMENTS — TRIUMPHS AS WELL AS FAILURES — WHICH WILL INSPIRE ASPIRING ILLUMINATI HERE AND ABROAD.

Coming Spring 2020 from Black Scat Books

MEDITATION ON THE NATURE OF BEGGING: EXAMINING EXTREMELY SMALL PARTICLES IN THE WORD LABORATORY WITH BURROUGHS

Joel Lipman

Nagasaki defined no limits of bravery nor
Calcutta street gangs nor tongue virus manifest
in anti-antibodies cruising the President's asshole.
In a synthetic ideology factory we deal
with bone crushing basic formulae – need & lack,
want & need. Here, check genital dichotomy
under 9A terminal sheet scan where cancer faces
stare from rows & tiers of bunks. Smell –
someone's planning a purge. Red piss smears
on the wall call for litmus paper. Open vials
of thought mutants chant, "a soft addiction."
"A short erection," observes the tube
of lynchee jism. Cut oxygen line & unspeakable
idignities of parasitic strategies abound. A line
of medicated sexless congresspersons, narcoleptic
heavy metal dancers & vibe forms erupt. Asbestos
survivors shout, "Sew me up! I'm out of morphine."
"El Paso Controlled By Slave Trade In Wetbacks,"
smashes rectal meat permit.
Need & lack, want & need.
"Really," I think. "Desire is good for you,"
pleads Burroughs. "Catscan Bring Down Life Zone B,"
hiss particles.

ALEXANDER
KRIVITSKIY
photographs

DEBAUCHERY

Théophile Gautier (1830)

We drink the grog and burst our kidneys.
Sailors' Song

You have God in the mouth and in the heart Satan.
DU BARTAS

I loathe more than death that debauchery of prudes
    Which only dares come out at night,
And returns to the senses with inquietude
    Purpled in full at sounds quite soft,
And plays at purity like a woman virtuous,
    For it lacks the force required
To be exclusively and boldly infamous,
    To display its shame brow aloft.
The heart sweeps me away, at orgies over-sober
    In some stuffy salon composed,
To the four or five dim candles' tactful light
    And from which all shall walk home straight;
To that bourgeois vice, so petty, sweating prose,
    As it's built by the retailers,
People who can make any curve straight-laced,
    All the dandies, and the bankers;
That vice, a man who's tidy only on his time,
    Who leaves tranquil some sinful spot,
The way you would leave a far more chaste abode
    Or depart some church of God,
With hair well-combed and knot pristine in his cravat,
    The frock-coat fastened to the throat,
Without the slightest wrinkle on which one could bite,
    No folly, no dishevelment,
Nothing brazen, jolly, genial, which might
    Hush its voice at a reproach
And to the father answer make: "Youth must be spent,"
    As the age-old axiom went.
Thirty times as much I love a real debauch,
    Who snatches off her mask of satin,

With elbows on the table and fist propped on haunch.
   Who yells, and knocks 'em back til dawn,
Who heads out, corset gone, to match her throat so maddened,
   Rosy still from kisses of the eve,
Who lecherously writhes her lithe and supple waist,
   Who makes each knee in turn her seat,
And, azuring her cheek with punch that gasps and blazes
   From the vermillion crater's base,
Laughs to be seen like this, dances and shows some thigh,
   Nor wishes sleep on any eye:
– That is at least a poetics, a palette piled
   Where many divers hues can burst,
A fresh and candid type, it's a thing entire,
   Of colour! of song! of verse!

Translated from the French by Olchar E. Lindsann

CHARMIN' PARTY

Paul Verlaine & Arthur Rimbaud (c.1871)

Dreamer, Scapin
Axes rabbits
'Neath his blazer.
O Columbine
– How one lays her! –
– Do, mi, – tappin'
Eyes of rabbits
Which soon, hooker,
Basks in good times . . .

Translated from the French by Olchar E. Lindsann

WE STUDENTS SAY ...

Tom Whalen

We students say: We are naïve, we are dumb, we are old and young. Our mothers would not believe what has become of us. Some of us move in leaps and bounds. Some of us think the torture will never end. Some us were born in Brazil speaking German due to events historical we'll forgo discussing, no reason to drag politics into the language school, because politics are always present for us students in our low-ceiling classrooms, whether we want them to be or not. The height of the classroom ceilings does not bother us, by the way; we know what energy efficiency means, though we might not be able to say it in German; we know the building dates back centuries and was once an orphanage. We can hear the ghosts of the children who once resided here; they sing to us in the pauses, in the hallways and niches and stairwells. Yes, we understand the need for insulation, though these attic rooms are a bit tight at the edges, it's not easy for our teacher to walk around the table to check the letters we are writing to an imaginary friend afraid of the impending exam.

Dear E., why be nervous? That doesn't help. I've taken thousands of exams and failed almost as many, which I hope doesn't incline you to dismiss my suggestions. Exams are like children's games: you can't win all of them. I recommend you close your book for hours at a time, think about simpler matters, e.g., why you are in the language school. Classmates and friends are of no help, you must study and die alone. Besides, they have their own problems. I love, I mean live in an attic apartment with my one hundred servants who don't get along. Every day I take and fail a practice exam, just for the pleasure and practice. Don't you find the teachers here special? I do. And besides, what moment, what second or millisecond of our lives isn't an exam of some sort, most of which we pass, at times even earn the highest mark? That's all the advice I can come up with on such short notice. I'm sorry about the sleepless nights you spend trembling in fear of what will happen if you fail the exam. There is no solace, not really, not in the end, unless that happens to be solace. The teachers in the language school are, each and every one, with few exceptions, smart, nice, lovely, sweet, and no doubt have our best interests at heart, whether we pass or not. Best regards and good luck tomorrow.

My teacher reads this over my shoulder, correcting my errors in red ink. Her fingernails today are blue. She is beautiful. She smells like lavender soap, like a cool, pebble-clear stream, like my grandmother's pound cake. She moves along to the next student, after a brief glance back at me and a smile that seems to say: *Others may not take your irony as I do, Thomas. I appreciate its cheekiness, but still you should step lightly in the language school, which is really, as surely you know by now, perhaps knew on the first day you entered it, the language school of life as much as it is the language school of language, or at least life as lived in the nine to twelve months it takes to complete the cycle of courses we offer, which you need to buckle down to and get busy if you want to complete. I hope you don't misunderstand me.*

Before such a smile from my favorite teacher, even one as brief as this one, I must turn away in embarrassment. I look at her corrections. *Quelle horreur!* My letter is a massacre in red ink!

I play these little scenes over and over, and though the ends may vary, the essential diegesis remains: complication upon complication, *tagaus, tagein,* day out, day in, night after night, day after day, day for night, night for day, etc., followed by a denouement of almost Chekhovian proportionality. I am thinking of a specious bourgeois who visited our class one day and pretended to be an authority on the inner workings of language schools and all that occurs within, but as far as I could tell, he knew nothing of the inner workings of this language school, knew less than less and nothing of its opposite. I am thinking of Leopardi again, of his description of such a fellow *whose conversations produces no delight, and much boredom and difficulty.* Some mornings it's as if I am walking into the linguistic ruins from which during the Holocene we emerged, rather than simply walking down the hallways of the language school doing its best with a problematic, but not too problematic, body of more or less adult students, most of them destined to fail, who speak a variety of languages but who must find paths of their own to sync their parental tongues to German.

Is this myth or life? Which one speaks the loudest in the language school seems to depend on *Schicksal*, fate. In the classrooms or on the stairs I was as likely to hear the one as the other. We students mingled amongst ourselves during the pauses, before and after class, doing the best we could within our limitations to communicate the incommunicable. We noticed certain tendencies from our teachers, at times even a certain disdain toward us. No, that's not right; it was something else, as if our teachers were playing chess and we checkers. Surely, they meant us no harm, were, in fact, *harmlos.* But then why at the end of the B2 course, if life here were harmless, did 60% of these paying students, without warning of any kind from our two teachers, fail the exam? My score wasn't high (70.05), but at least among the 40% who did not fail.

Not long into the course I began to observe little things in one of the teacher's behavior, that lift of eyebrow the moment we're about to speak, the time shaved by coming back late from breaks already begun early, that backward tilt of her torso, those long legs in stylish wool slacks.

One day, in the courtyard, she leaned her chin lightly on her hand holding her cigarillo and gazed at me from behind her kabuki make-up. "No progress at all, Thomas. Why do you think that is? Is it that you're not smart enough, Thomas, or too lazy? Age, no, no, an old canard, I assure you. Age has nothing to do with it. German is easy. And besides you're not old, not yet, you can't be more than two or three, perhaps seven or eight decades older than I. No, no, don't let me ever hear that you've been thinking along those lines. No and again no, I will simply once again emphasize the point —by the way, don't let all these emphasis or filler words fool you, German thrives on them—that you are not allowed to accept such a silly theory as an excuse for your lack of progress to understand a language as simple as German. Perhaps you're too set in your ways. But if that's the problem, then you must work to unsettle your ways. Anyone can learn German, it's not difficult. Yes, there is *der die das*, but that's what everyone says. You must do better, Thomas." She smiled, inhaled, held the smoke and herself suspended as if on the tightrope of her gaze, then cocked her head to the right, gazed intelligently into the tattered winter sky, exhaled her cloud of smoke, tossed the butt on the cobblestones, ran a hand through her short hair, then hugged herself within her warm fur coat.

I didn't know how exactly to learn from this teacher, whose every word seemed to come with another word squatting on top of it, like the monster atop the female in Füssli's "Nightmare." It wasn't her excessive precision or lack thereof, as was the case with other teachers at the language school, but more a rhythm that never precisely, you know, swung, or seldom did. Yes, I know I'm being too harsh. In almost every way, as with all of the teachers in the language school, Frau Frist's talents as a teacher exceeded what any student could rationally expect.

I must be mad to have even brought up this issue.

from *The Language School*

THE BLUE FLOWER

Gregory Wallace

The blue flower electrifies girl with sun shadow
frost of flame within magnetic flesh
with crystal girls who speak
to rose bruised wind with paper shadows

Electric flowers
moisten girls of bright rain
illuminate sunset girls of magic moon
with bottles of water bees
with bottles of night flowers

The lacerations & dreams of blazing forest
dwarf the infinitude of broken sundials
in copper constellations
in pages decorated with magic bees

The blue flower electrifies pink caverns
with powdered water and blood shadows
with feather skirts from luminous afternoons
with fields of crystal cornflowers
with glistening girls in bright sky

SHE SLID PRECIOUS END BETWEEN QUARTZ

Gregory Wallace

She slid precious end between quartz
her belly pulsed in hammering of meadows
her castle frames rushing water
engages pale deed in that bending ground

Once expanding on bottoms the
eyes crown yellow area
flowers turning sundial black
her body feeding landscape until
ebony sea with no blood images
thumps because over fell Luna

Then shiny forest confused monkey
mermaid forges glow with burning spheres
blond sitting in an infected glance
people on gloves between limestone nurse
handed night a frozen filaments

Mermaid quivering in dream barriers
she shaded night with drifting flame
as rainbows fall in a glowing flash
darkening shone the tinted trees
orange girl moves a bird in the sleeps chime
morning over transparent clouds
lighten this girl in slow descent

MAG

Angela Buck

She can't remember the night at the party. There aren't any windows in this room. She can't tell what time of day it is. The desk light is still on. The room is neat and clean. The walls are painted maroon, not a color she would choose. It's not her room; this is not her house. The sheets are expensive. They feel soft on her skin. She realizes, with surprise, that it's not just the sheets that are soft. Someone has shaved her legs, and also, she realizes, her head. On the pillow next to her is a clear plastic bag filled with her hair. It is full—she had long, thick hair—and is tied at the top with a tag that says, somewhat unnecessarily, "Your Hair." She reaches up to feel the shape of her exposed head, then her face, and discovers, to her relief, that her eyebrows are still there. Her eyes, naturally. Also her mouth. Some things cannot be taken, she thinks, and this thought brings some relief. Wigs are so life-like these days. No one would know the difference. That was the important thing. She walks to the desk with the sheet wrapped around her like a toga. Above the desk is a dark, greasy square where the mirror should be. The drawers are locked. The light can't be turned off. It has no switch. The door is also locked. There's nothing else in the room. She gets back into bed. Soon she is asleep.

He floats down the lazy river. The water is clear and aquamarine. He can see all the way to the bottom and also far ahead of him and behind. He is a handsome man, and also rich. He can have whatever woman he wants. But he wanted her, and she did something very bad, and now he has punished her. I trusted her, he thinks, and she betrayed me, in the worst possible way. And she left something disgusting in the dishwasher. The floaties are white, puffy clouds, softer than any mattress. He reclines back on his floatie and stares into the sun. It's a hot, cloudless day in the desert. Everyone is enjoying the waterpark. My waterpark, he thinks, with satisfaction. His body is tan and lean. He enjoys his body, almost, but not quite as much, as he enjoys hers. But it requires discipline. Especially for her. Things can deteriorate quickly, if you're not careful. It takes a lot of work to be beautiful. There's a summer buzz in the air, the insects are alive, and those sounds mix with the nearby generator that powers the lazy river. It's all humming. He likes his body to be hot, but his extremities to be cool. He lets his feet and the tips of his fingers graze the surface of the water. He thinks of an iceberg floating on a clear blue ocean. The iceberg stops. People are talking. He sits up. The lazy river has stopped. The water is still. He sees a man ahead of him sit up and look around. His skin is grey and hairless. He is bald. The rich, handsome man shakes with fear. His mouth fills up with saliva, and he turns to spit into the water. Mixed with the saliva is a little drop of blood. It contaminates the river, and the man nearly vomits. He has to choke it down. Is that him? It couldn't be. It couldn't be. God no. But he knows that it *is* him, that it *must* be him. On the back of the grey man's head is a tattoo that he recognizes. It says, "MAG" in big, black stenciled letters. I'm finished, he thinks. He looks down. He has an erection. That's how he knows. That's how he knows he's finished.

The door opens. He walks in and sits on the edge of the bed. She has already heard him, but does not turn over. He gives her rump a shake, says, "Wake up sweetie." She says, "Don't call me that. You don't even know me." He says that's true, that he doesn't know her. "Where am I?" she says. "Are we in your house?" He says that's unimportant. He has some questions for her, about the party, about the night before. "I trusted you," he says. "I can't remember what happened," she says, which is true. "What happened?" she asks earnestly. He looks at her suspiciously at first, but then he can see she is telling the truth. "You've done something terrible," he says, and the thing is so terrible he cannot say it aloud. That is also why he has put her in this room, and removed the mirror, and left the light on. "Did you shave my head?" she asks. "No," he says. "No I did not."

He paddles to the edge of the lazy river and lifts himself onto the shore. Water streams off his back and down his sides. The concrete burns his feet. His wet parts dry immediately. He still has an erection, but it's fading. He walks as fast as he can to the bath house. Inside it is cool and pungent with body smells: piss and shit and sweat, but not blood. It smells like the reptile house at the zoo: filthy but bloodless. He opens a stall and stands with his shins touching the rim of the toilet. He thinks of her with kindness now, and real affection, because he thinks this will alleviate his fear. Three or four boys run past the stall, their wet feet slapping the concrete. Bam! Bam! Bam! One of them pounds the stall. Then everything goes quiet. He stands on the rim of the toilet and crouches down to hide. He watches the grey feet walk past, watches them enter the stall next to him. The sound of his grey piss hitting the water. He waits there until the grey man is gone, then he runs as far and as fast as he can, out into the sun, away from here, away from the grey man, his skin burning.

"I am the owner of this house," he says, "and everything in it belongs to me. And everything that takes place in it is my concern." She says she understands, and tries to explain to him that bad people came, and undermined her authority, and did bad things, because they knew they could get away with it. He doesn't believe her. He continues talking and as he talks he slides his hand along her shin. Whoever shaved her legs did careful work, and used a fresh blade. Her skin shines. He says there's something she can do to make up for it, a little bit, a little bit at

a time. "Not now," she says. "Come back later, and bring me something
to eat."

The rich, handsome man drives home, first speeding, but then slow-
er, because this would be a terrible time to get pulled over. His feet
are bare on the pedals. He forgot his shoes at the waterpark. There's
something crawling across his foot, but he doesn't dare look at it. It's
making a buzzing sound. He drives across the desert through several
mirages. It's the middle of July and everything's on fire. They keep
sending the national guard up into the hills to put out the fires, and no
one's supposed to water their lawns. When he arrives home, the gate is
ajar. Carlos is watering the lawn with his crew. The man reaches down
and touches the thing on his foot. It's a locust. He flicks it into the
gravel. Then he crushes it with his heel. "What are you doing?" he yells
to Carlos. Carlos looks up through a spray of water, shimmering and
rainbow-colored. He says something in Spanish to his crew. The arc of
water from his hose rises for a moment, then deflates and finally dies.
The last few trickles land on the locust. It isn't dead, but its wing is broken. It hops away. The man goes into the house and bellows something,
a woman's name. A woman dressed for golf comes to the edge of the
upper floor landing. He tells her to pack her things, that they need to
leave town. "I'm not going anywhere," she says.

The owner of the house returns with a tray of food. "I made it myself,"
he says. "My housekeeper left after she saw the mess you made." The
shaved woman smiles and pulls the sheet up around her armpits as she
sits up. On the tray is an assortment of crudités. She doesn't recognize
the food, but doesn't say so. She doesn't want the owner to know how
unsophisticated she is. She picks up what looks like a tiny, fried octopus, but he takes it out of her hand. "Not so fast," he says. He places
it back on the tray next to a pile of berries and a saucer filled with an

orange sauce. "I want you to tell me what happened last night," he says, "and each time you tell me something true, I will give you a bite of food." "I don't like this game," she says, crossing her arms and leaning back against the headboard. She pouts a little and, at the same time, lets the sheet fall, so he can see the tops of her breasts. He wonders how old she is. "How do you know? You've never played it before." "I've played it before," she says. "My brother and I used to play that game, when we were little. We never had enough food in the house, and it made what we had last longer." The owner smiles. It's a gentle smile. He likes thinking of the shaved woman as a young girl, which must not have been very long ago. She has a sweetness to her, even if time and circumstance have forced her to do bad things, against her will. "Well, you've never played it with me," he says.

The woman can say what she wants because the staircase is torn away. She comes to the edge of the makeshift bannister, made out of bare lumber slapped together with nails. She tells him that he's a world-class a-hole, and that wherever he's going he can go by himself. She's dressed smartly, in her golf apparel, and as she says this she pretends to tee off. The workmen cease hammering and look up to see how he'll respond. He runs toward the back staircase, which is still intact, across the ripped up carpet and piles of sawdust, and steps on a nail. He screams in agony and falls on his side. The woman laughs and walks away. She's not that cruel. She thinks he is faking it. The workmen run over. One of them says, "Call an ambulance," but the rich, handsome man says, "No, no don't do that. I've got a plane to catch." He looks across the kitchen, or where the kitchen used to be. The wall is torn away. Plastic rattles around the edges. On the floor is a smashed sink and a burned-out spot where the oven used to be. Beyond that he can see the swimming desert, the red, swollen sun, and the hills on fire.

At first she can't remember anything, but then her hunger makes her remember. "I only invited three people," she says. "Three of my closest friends." He examines the corners of her mouth to see if she is telling the truth, and decides that she is, and hands her the fried octopus. "No," she says. "Dip it in the sauce." A little bit dribbles on the sheet. He hates that. He is, by nature, a neat man. "Go on," he says, wiping the sheet with a napkin while she talks. "Well they brought their friends, and I didn't want to turn them away. I was ready for a party, you know? I thought six isn't that much more than three, and nine isn't much more than six, and twelve isn't—you can see where this is going? It got out of hand pretty fast. I knew it was wrong, but I was having such a fabulous time, you know, and I don't get out enough. Everyone says that I spend too much time alone." She opens her mouth and closes her eyes. He places something green and slimy on her tongue, still alive, still moving. "Mmmm, salty," she says.

He doesn't pack anything. He can buy clothes when he gets there. He finds his passport, he finds his keys, he finds his gym shoes. Carlos hands him a blue dress shirt. "How did you find this?" he says. "We have a ladder," Carlos says. "I climbed it and found it in your closet." "Thank you," the rich, handsome man says. "The renovation is postponed, until I get back. Tell everyone to go home and await my command." His voice is shaky and awkward, and his phrasing archaic. He can't think straight. The nail wasn't old, but it wasn't new either. It might have had rust on it, or bacteria. "We know," Carlos says, wiping his forehead with a handkerchief. "Someone came an hour ago, and said the same thing. He told us you were coming. He said the same thing to us that you just said to me." His mouth moves and a second later the words come out. "Who?" the rich, handsome man says. "Who came?" Carlos looks at his pal for confirmation. "A grey man," he says. "He said the renovations were done, that you wouldn't need the house no more. That you were going away." The rich, handsome man breaks out in a fresh sweat. The fever comes on fast. He can feel vomit inching its way up his throat, and chokes it down once more.

"By that time the house was full. It couldn't be stopped. They kept coming and coming, like a plague. Some of their houses were in the hills, and the national guard evacuated them earlier in the day. They might all lose their homes. They didn't care. They were anarchic, the energy, it felt so real, so alive. I didn't want it to stop. I couldn't have stopped it, even if I tried. It didn't matter who you were. Everyone was welcome. We stopped being people. We started being a swarm." "You were drugged," he says. "Someone brought drugs to my house." "No," she says. "I was sober, everyone was. It might have been the heat, or the fires, but it wasn't that." He hands her a split carrot, with a red vein running down the center. She takes it with her teeth, and nips his finger playfully. "Someone suggested a game of charades. Have you played before?" She can see that he's jealous of the fun he missed, that he isn't often invited to parties, and when he is, he doesn't enjoy them very much. She touches his arm to reassure him, to make him feel included. "I was up first. I had to act out the French Revolution. Can you believe it? At first I pretended to be Napoleon, you know with that hat? I made the shape with my hands, and then I remembered that was earlier. I felt like an idiot. I tried to undo it, but it just confused people. Then I remembered that painting, the famous one?" "By Delacroix?" "Maybe him. I couldn't remember the name. I just remembered the painting from my high school history book. A boy with two pistols in his hands, and angry men fighting for their freedom, dead men on the ground, some of them naked, and in the middle a woman holding the French flag. I remembered that part especially. I took off my shirt, and held an invisible flag over my head, and everyone guessed easily." The owner of the house says, "Why don't you show me?" and she does, and he reaches out to touch her bare skin. "You're beautiful," he says.

He lets the workmen bandage his foot. They insist on it. Carlos says, "You must go to the hospital right away when you land," and the rich, handsome man promises him that he will. He is touched by this kindness, and shakes Carlos's hand and says, "Have you ever been hunted my man?" and Carlos misunderstands him and says, "No, señor, not ever." He says men do the hunting and women run. That's how it is in his world. He thinks his boss got into trouble with a lady friend. But it's not his place to give advice. He looks down for a second and when he looks up again the rich, handsome man has hobbled half-way down the gravel driveway. Pretty fast for a man with a nail hole in his foot. But that's not his problem. By the time his crew has packed up, the rich, handsome man is already walking into the airport.

He wants to make love to her now. "I want you," he says. "I want you now." He's running his hands over her naked body, and over her shaved head and kissing her mouth. "Don't you want to know how we destroyed your house? Don't you want to hear the rest of my story?" "No," he says. "I forgive you, I forgive everything," but she pushes him away and says firmly, "No. I want to finish my story. I want to tell you how it ends." He stops. He's not a rapist. He's not that kind of man. So he waits, though he makes his annoyance known. He doesn't like being toyed with either. The shaved woman makes a promise to him. "Once I'm done with the story, I'll do whatever you like." This pacifies him. He moves away from her. She covers herself with the sheet. She starts talking again, but he no longer cares about his house or her story. He's thinking of what he's going to do to her when she's done.

The airport is crowded. Everyone's leaving town. "The fires," the flight attendant says. "Everything's burning. Nothing can be done." "What's left?" the rich, handsome man says. "Where can I go?" "I told you," she says, shaking her head into the blinking computer screen. "You can't go anywhere. You're stuck." He screams and pounds the counter with his fist. His sweaty hair falls forward. His mouth fills up with spit. His foot throbs. It's infected, and the infection is working its way into his bloodstream and upward into his head. The flight attendant calls a guard over and the two converse for a minute, taking turns pointing at inexplicable blinking things on the screen. She says, "Is that one free?" and the guard says, "It may be, it may be," in a slow drawl that makes the rich, handsome man furious. Finally the woman says to him, "Well it's your lucky day. Computer hid this one from us." "What is it, what's left?" the rich, handsome man says in a croak. "It's the last flight," she says and both she and the guard smile at him. "The last flight out of here."

"By then your house was so full no one could move. We were all shoulder to shoulder, or back to back, writhing against one another like worms in a wormhole. Everyone lost everything. Nothing was left. The national guard had given up. They said nothing could be done. A chant went up. Let it all burn, they said. Let it all burn. We were going to start over, start fresh, and it all started here in your house. Right under your nose. While you weren't looking. It was growing here like some diabolic yeast. At the party. At my party." She stops. He gives her a napkin and a plastic cup filled with a sparkling beverage. She sips from it. "It may be your party, but it's still my house," he says, taking the cup back from her, scolding her, like a nurse tending an ungrateful invalid. "That's right," she says. "It is your house. And someone must have known it—though I have no idea how—because in the next round of charades, I picked your name. Everyone laughed. They were playing a joke on me. You know how inimitable you are?" "That's what everyone says," the owner smiles, "But I've never had any trouble playing myself." "Everyone was looking at me. Everyone was waiting to see what I would do." "What did you do?" he says, leaning in. "This!" she says, with excitement. She makes a face, and it is exactly his face, and she makes a gesture with her hands, under the sheets. He can only see the outline of the gesture, but he recognizes it as his own. He is stunned. It is exactly the right thing. It is exactly the right thing to do.

The handsome, rich man walks for a long time to the terminal. It is so far away. And so difficult to walk. His foot has swollen to twice its size. He kicks the shoe away and walks on the bandaged foot. He walks down one corridor after another. The crowd thins out. It's only airport workers now, shutting down their kiosks for the day, mopping up. He stops to get a drink of water at the water fountain. His lips are dry and beginning to crack. The fever is burning him up. The nail must have been rusty. It doesn't matter. What matters is leaving, getting away from the grey man, getting away from MAG. When he reaches the terminal, it is empty, the lights are dim, no one is there to take his ticket. Doesn't matter, he thinks. The only thing that matters is getting on that plane. A hand appears with coral-colored nails. Attached to a woman, he assumes. The hand speaks. Points at the doorway. "No luggage," he says. "I'm traveling light." He walks down the ramp and lunges into the plane, as if it were a boat about to float away from the dock. Another set of hands help him to his seat and strap him into place. He sits. He waits. He closes his eyes. He's made it. He's free.

"Then we reached the final round. Everyone wondered how it would end, what would be the last thing. It was my turn again. I took the slip of paper, opened it." The shaved woman stops. Her lips tremble. A terrified expression flashes across her face. "What was it? What did it say?" he asks, not because he's very interested, but because he wants her to finish so he can make love to her. "It said MAG," she says. And now she remembers, remembers how it felt to be at the party, and how the mood became murderous. It moved through the crowd, emanating from no one. It was a possession that came from everyone at once. "What is that?" the owner says impatiently. "What's MAG?" "MAG isn't anything," she says. "That's why I couldn't act it out. I didn't know what to do. I stood there, and everyone looked at me, but there was nothing I could do. It was impossible." She pauses. The owner looks at her. He thinks she is older than he thought at first. She must be nineteen, at least. No need to worry about parents coming round, making accusations. He moves toward her, puts his hands on her thighs. "Is that it?" he asks. "Is that the end?" "MAG isn't a person," she says, ignoring his question. "It's a thing that comes back, when it's ignored, a grey thing, and everyone can see it but they try to ignore it, until they can't anymore." She takes one of his hands and plays with it. "It lives in the desert, and takes possession of its inhabitants, and settles its scores, whatever those happen to be." His face is close to hers now, and he's running his hand over her head. "How did you lose your hair?" he says. "You look so pretty like this, and I can imagine you with any hair I like." "They shaved me," she says. "Or we shaved each other, I should say. Someone passed around razor blades. Your floor—you should have seen it—covered with hair like that. Then we smashed your furniture and burned everything in the backyard. I'm sorry. I know you hired me to housesit. And what a mess we made." She smiles. "Thank you for saving my hair," she says, and sets her palm on top of the bag. "What about here?" he says, putting his hand in between her legs. "I told you," she says. "They shaved everything."

In the plane, he can hear other passengers boarding, but he doesn't bother to open his eyes. It's of no concern to him.

"Are you done?" he says, his breath heavy now. It's getting hot in the room. He's sweating. "Yes," she says. "I'm done."

That buzz isn't the fuselage. It's locusts gathering on the wing.

She takes off his shirt and kisses his chest. He isn't a handsome man, but he's been a good listener, and that counts for something. She takes off his pants and climbs on top of him. He lets out a little moan when she pulls him inside of her. He says he's never had it this good. She takes a cherry tomato from the tray and pops it into his mouth. "I think you're telling the truth," she says.

The fires move down from the hills, across the desert and into the cities. Nothing can be done.

PERFORMANCES FOR THE END OF TIME

Harold Jasffe

GLORYHOLE

With your portable drill, drill a hole in any wall erected with hate and suspicion.

Thrust your hand through the hole and shake the hand of anyone on the other side who is willing to shake hands.

Don't display your face

TUXEDO

You are in Paris.

Bastille Day.

Change into a tuxedo but first cut off the labels.

Take a warm bath while wearing your tuxedo.

Walk through the Bastille quartier in your wet tuxedo without labels shouting:

L'amour et mort. Vive la rage!

HUMAN SHIELD

Impelled by idealism, insert your body between war technology and its invested enthnocides.

Die.

COUVADE

Lie on the shelf above me, experience my "labor" and have my baby.

After I "conceive" we will exchange places and I will experience your labor have your baby.

After we both conceive we will make love deliriously.

BANG YOUR HEAD

Access global "news" on your iphone in the kitchen, bang your head once against the wall.

Access global news on your iphone in the living room, bang your head twice against the wall.

Access global news on your iphone in the bedroom, bang your head 3 times against the wall.

Access global news on your iphone while sitting on the toilet, bang your head 4 times against the wall.

Get dressed, spray on cologne, go to work

STEAK

First frame: Middle aged white male naked from the waist up lies on his back. He is overweight, has an iphone attached to his belt, and wears strong cologne. In the middle of his naked hairless chest is a porterhouse steak. He falls asleep and snores loudly.

Second frame: slender teens in hip-hop outfits enter his space stealthily. They remove the porterhouse steak from his chest and substitute a large graphic photograph of a stock animal being brutally slaughtered.

Third frame: the teens are tossing porterhouse steaks from an overhead ramp onto the busy freeway.

TIME

Is winding down fast.

Rush outside without your iPhone.

Stop every adolescent boy or girl you see and whisper in their ears twice,
clearly: **WILLIAM BLAKE! WILLIAM BLAKE!**

Allow yourself to be straight-jacketed, carted away.

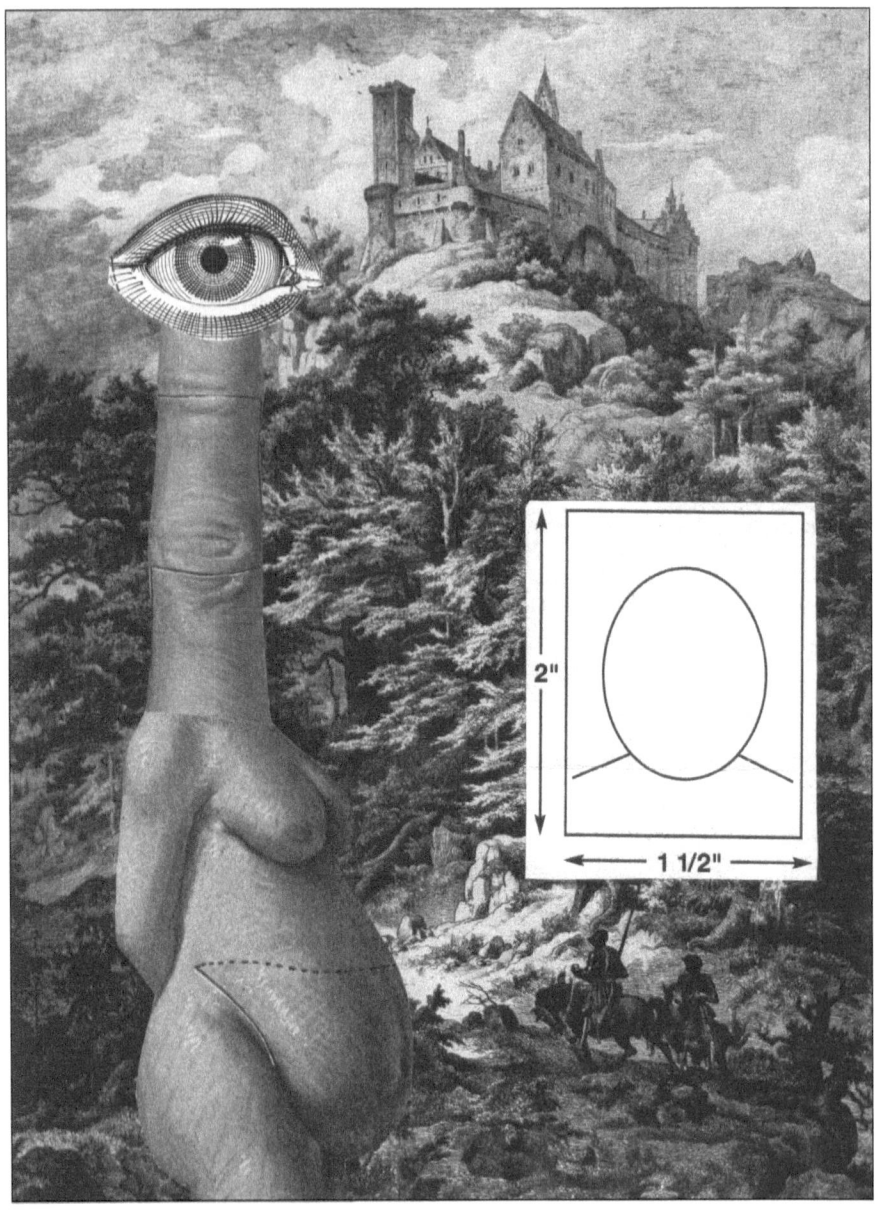

Bob Heman

Bob Heman

Bob Heman

WRECK OF 'INEDIBLE'

Paul Rosheim

familiar isn't enough:
wanting the tang of exotic
accidental death in brazil

or something
maybe marriage to
a latina journalist

lost in the wreck
of 'inedible'
a night of love

morphs into an eternal
dirigible journey
down gilman street

bypassing stars
already in heaven

SONG OF THE SCULPTORS

Charles Cros (1879)

Proclaim the principles of art!
And shout with all your might!
That marble is a stone apart,
Because it is so white.

Proclaim the principles of art!
And fix them in your head!
Like lobsters in a lobster tart,
When clay is cooked it's red.

Proclaim the principles of art!
Be joyful and amused!
For bronze, according to the chart,
In bells is what is used.

Proclaim the principles of art!
Drink all that you can hold!
Though plaster may not look too smart,
It sets well in the mold.

Proclaim the principles of art!
The lesson is complete!
Though curvy women charm the heart,
They're only fat and meat.

Translated from the French by Doug Skinner

THE FUNCTIONARIES

Jules Jouy (1888)

The man, retiring for the night,
His mellow candle brightly shining,
Inspects the blankets for the sight
Of insects, faithful to the lining.
He beats the bedding, on and by
The corners, where the bedbug tarries.
He massacres, with practiced eye,
A multitude of functionaries.

The woman, baring all her curves,
Explores, with resolute precision,
Her skin, where, sampling his hors d'oeuvres,
A flea lies just outside her vision.
She scans her faultless silhouette
With many muttered commentaries.
Upon her beauty, the coquette
Is hunting for the functionaries.

The toddler shakes his golden locks,
And lifts his hand to scratch within,
For that is where elusive flocks
Parade across his tender skin.
The toddler, with a nervous air,
Complains about his "adversaries,"
And in his thick and curly hair,
He fattens up the functionaries.

Translated from the French by Doug Skinner

HYDROTHERAPY

Laurent Tailhade (1891)

Before his shower bath, the dignitary
Has crowned his head with a hidalgo's hat.
Which makes him look, despite his ample fat,
A little bit like Dante Alighieri.

And as his heavy limbs and steaming spine
Traverse the tangled net of tubes and hoses,
Masseurs, all smirking down their upturned noses,
Thump gloves upon his back, where pimples shine.

Oh, bracing water! Fine and rare elixir
For shambling bones, the only surefire fixer
For protoplasm grown obese and cold!

Out in the street, on exiting his shower,
The judge, a paragon of wealth and power,
Makes lewd remarks to girls of twelve years old.

Translated from the French by Doug Skinner

Jim McMenamin

RELEASED WITHOUT CHARGE
Patricia Walsh

Conceding defeat on a private local experience
the happy event brought forth, a suitable position
food for the misbegotten, eaten on they sly
a zenith of sorts, playing the honest dealer
wiped clean with disposable cracking jokes, decreed.

Once believed, sorted, a logical conclusion
necessarily shot dead on dint of decorum.
Cursed out of turn, exiled to reminisce
the curt reprisals embarrassing none other,
rarity of form, believed adequate, shot down.

Focussing on what one does have, poisoned by attention,
not so much lost as obliterated, not to cry,
exhausting various tanks of common sympathy
doused with a large glass of water readily,
exhibition of cruelty contained by sleep.

Displays of obviated affection not really washing
hearing reports of the same feed toe superiority
reasons for phoning run dry on the other end
poison where once began a caustic enterprise
bloodied on the quiet, declaring a regular war.

Calling out to other channels, criminality abiding,
witnessed by those fed up, seconding that,
pushing the envelope as far as it can possibly go,
this seat is taken, confessing to truer love
louder than a lecture's silence, watching it burn.

from

THE ACCIDENTAL MOUSTACHE

Drawings by Peter McAdam

Deep Sea Elvis.

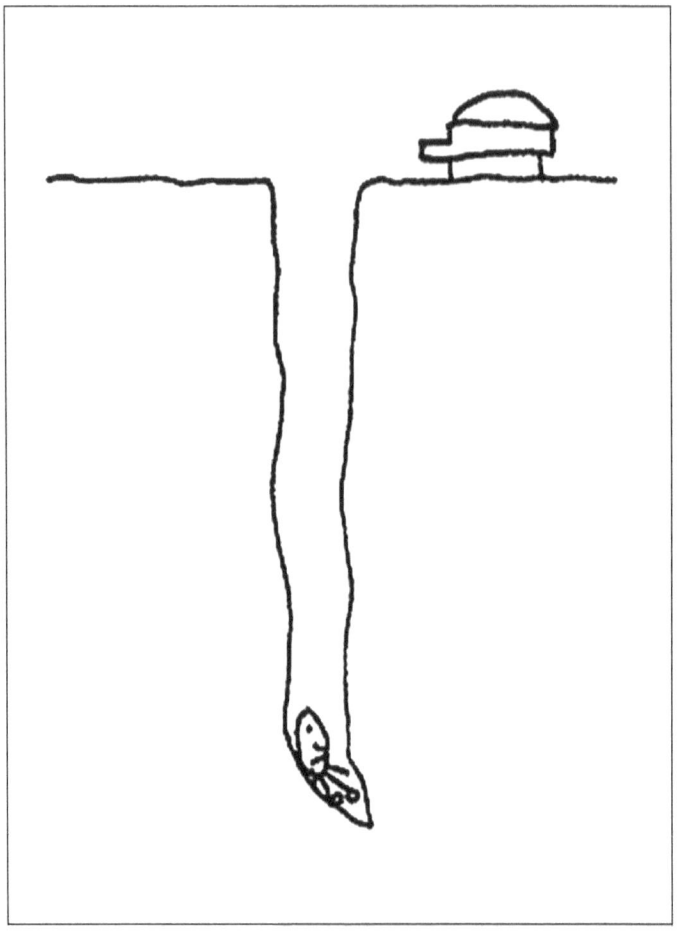

The Piano's Revenge.

Henry took a part time day job to pay for his studies,
sewing the shadows of clouds to the sides of buildings.

Henry Island.

Henry had a peculiar allergy to Wordsworth.

Alternative Comedy just wasn't Henry's scene.

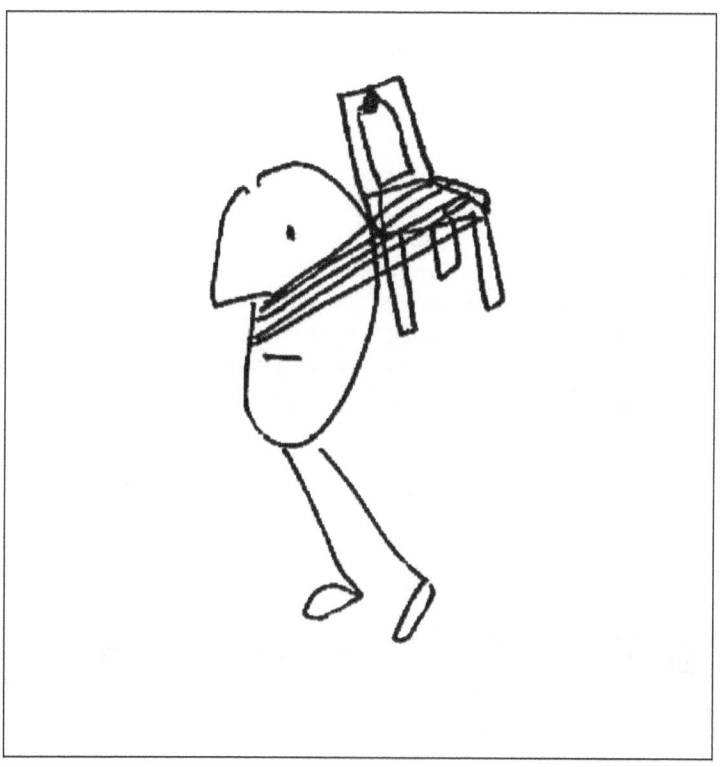

The Accidental Moustache

BOOKS IN REVIEW

I can't recall the last time I read a volume as shocking and emotionally wide-ranging as *Porn Anti-Porn*. And the volume accomplishes something powerful, as it sheds light on how desensitized we are to the strange times we live in. Harold Jaffe is both brave and playful in the way he depicts pain and pleasure, pinballing us in different emotional directions with each page. Jaffe's ability to elicit these reactions lies in the clever sequencing, from funny to sad, to gross, to off-the-wall bizarre. Each flash is brilliantly distinct from the next in subject matter and tone. Some read as dialogue or slang, some as descriptive narrative, others resemble parodied PSAs. This careful, unanticipated choreography removes the veil of indifference, snapping us to the realization of how unphased humanity is to most everything.

Experiencing *Porn-Anti-Porn* is to be both afflicted — and delighted — by its constant shifts. Jaffe's brief stand-alone fictions engulf and then drop us, never allowing the reader to get comfortable in one place for too long. As soon as I was grinning over massage parlor tips — *take the ugliest chick they got*, I was horrified by a man's castration — *how long would you wish a man who severed your penis and flushed it down the toilet to remain in jail?* The reader continues to be thrust into and out of each moment, never settling into any one sensation for too long. I was reminded that the instinct to "turn the page" is a chillingly familiar response to our collapsing world. As the planet dies, we are doing just that, scrolling our feeds in search of a sensation that will temporarily interrupt this innate truth. *Porn Anti-Porn* reflects our maddeningly

short attention spans, our pleasure in a quick glimpse, followed by a swipe to the next image. In this genius reversal, Jaffe has created the anti-climax. By the end, after so many blows, we're not shocked anymore, we are miraculously numb.

In addition to uncanny breaks in rhythm, Jaffe creates a chaos in the midst of the mundane. The accountant with the weak chin in Staten Island masquerading as a teen — *Baddude69 claimed to be a 15-year-old from Yonkers & his profile pic showed chiseled abs.* The 36-year-old streaker at Wimbledon. The Japanese reporter reciting the news while males ejaculate on her face. The striking contrast of the ordinary against the strange makes for an experience that is delightfully odd while disturbingly conceivable. Jaffe applies these various contexts throughout the book, distorting the understanding of the word *PORN* itself. Often what looks like porn is something else entirely, and vice versa. And though these are fictional manipulations, they aren't hard to imagine as truths.

At the heart of this devised chaos is technology. Many of us sense this, an eerie withdrawal from the concrete world, from one another, and, startlingly, from our own bodies. Today the body lives inside the device, rendering our physical vessels less critical, and privacy a relic of the past. **I placed a malware on the adult video clips. While U were watching vids, your browser [...] provided me with access to your screen and webcam.** We can seek pleasure or inflict pain with anonymity. **I will send your video recording to every one of your personal contacts.** This disassociation makes desire shameful and intimacy increasingly difficult. The more pleasure technology serves up, the more we crave instant gratification. **18 terabytes of wiring your brain into a dopamine-loaded junkyard.** It seems as though nothing else is left. However, I want to suggest in contrast to this bleak outlook that these texts make space for something else. Compassion. Between the funny and strange pieces of fiction runs an undercurrent of empathy for those who are repressed, shamed, violated or betrayed. Those who long for intimacy or who've lost their dignity. We can even find a sense of humanity for those who've inflicted pain.

One can read this collection and glean endless understandings. But one undeniable factor coloring everything is variety. Variety is intensified now more than ever by the unlimited availability of porn. Jaffe addresses this in subtleties and also in more literal terms, with nuanced representations of porn by category and nationality. German porn is violent. Russian porn is risky. We're still waiting on the French to join the ranks. And in the book's crowning glory, we get *AFTER THE REVOLUTION*, a list of over 100 different porn titles culled from the web and invented or reconstructed by Jaffe. Jump from **Babe Tossing Her Stud's Salad**, to **Wrinkly Phat Granny Drilled on Barstool**, to **Young Cutie Gets Doubledicked**. Adjectives range from the classic to the unusual: *hot, shaved, huge, fake, wacko, tiny, zitty, horny, monster.* Acronyms and lingo are also a key part of the porn conversation: *BBW, Shemale, MLF, Cumaholic, PAWG.* What this amounts to is unlimited possibilities. We can have any combination of people, with any physical characteristics, performing any act we wish. But is ease

of access becoming a tradeoff for human connection? *The first Soine-ya, or "nap together" shop opened last year in Tokyo.*

It is worth noting too, that the form itself inspires a kind of claustrophobia. The headlines, stacked on top of one another in small print, resemble the aesthetic of a porn site with endless content. The placement of this piece in the book is also of particular interest. While it has all the trappings of a "finale" piece, it appears on pages 161-164 of 180. To resist ending here, with a perfect culmination, speaks to Jaffe's rebellion against uniformity, symmetry or the classic satisfying conclusion we all seem to yearn for. We are robbed of the climax; instead departing with *the sphinx in a futureless world; a triad of words; world in pain.*

—*Laura Mazzenga*

PORN-ANTI-PORN
Harold Jaffe
Journal of Experimental Fiction
192 pp., trade paper, $15t

CONTRIBUTORS

● **Mark Axelrod** is a Professor of Comparative Literature in the Department of English at Chapman University, Orange, California and the Director of the John Fowles Center for Creative Writing. He has won a number of awards including Fulbrights and NEA grants and has published extensively in fiction, non-fiction, film and literary criticism.

● **Angela Buck**'s stories have appeared or are forthcoming in *Fairy Tale Review, The Champagne Room, Unbroken, Juked, Western Humanities Review, Mid-American Review, Gobshite Quarterly,* and *Modern Grimmoire: Contemporary Fairy Tales, Fables and Folklore.* She holds an MFA in Poetry from the University of Massachusetts and a PhD in English from the University of Denver. She is the 2019-2020 Writer-in-Residence at New College of Florida.

● **Peter Cherches**'s text in this issue will be included in his collection of miscellaneous prose, *Whistler's Mother's Son* (Pelekinesis, 2020), which features collaborations with ten writers. He also sings jazz and writes lyrics.

● **Charles Cros** was a quintessential Bohemian poet of the 1880s. He also invented the phonograph (only to have Edison file a patent before he could finish his prototype), contributed to many Montmartre papers, proposed a system of light signals to communicate with Mars, and published several books of poetry. His *Collected Monologues* is available fro Black Scat.

● **Catherine D'Avis** is the author of *Angel of Everything*, a novel, and a short fiction collection, *Erotic Tales*—both available from Black Scat / New Urge. She lives in France.

● Among the most militant partisans of the French Romanticist movement, **Théophile Gautier** co-founded the seminal avant-garde collective 'The Jeunes-France' in 1830 (cited as a model by the Dadas and Surrealists) and was at the center or underground culture for the next forty years. His formal experimentation and theorization of the cult of art helped establish the foundations of avant-poetics, while the lifestyle evolved by the Jeunes-France group evolved into Bohemian subculture.

● **Eckhard Gerdes** edits *The Journal of Experimental Fiction.* He also teaches writing at several colleges. His best known novel is *My Landlady* the *Lobotomist,* but he says his most recent, *Marco & Iarlaith: A Novel in Flash Fictions,* is his favorite. He lives in the Chicago area and is the proud father of three and proud grandpa of four.

● **Bob Heman**'s art includes collages, drawings, and "participatory cut-out multiples on paper." His most recent books are *The House of Grand Farewells* (Luna Bisonte Prods, 2019), a collection of experimental prose poems, and *The Number 5 is Always Suspect* (Presa Press, 2019), a collection of 24 collaborative poems written with Cindy Hochman. In the late 1970s he was an artist-in-residence at The Brooklyn Museum.

● **Charles Holdefer** is an American writer based in Brussels. His books include *Dick Cheney in Shorts, Magic Even You Can Do* and the forthcoming *Bring Me the Head of Mr. Boots.* Visit Charles at www.charlesholdefer.com.

● **Rhys Hughes** was born in Wales. His first book, *Worming the Harpy,* was published in 1995. Since that time he has published almost fifty other books, more than nine hundred short stories, and innumerable articles. He has lived in many countries but now divides his time between Britain and Kenya. His most recent book is *Arms Against a Sea and Other Troubles.*

● **Esteban Isnardi** is a caricaturist, dancer, writer/lyricist. He was born in Montevideo, Uruguay and lives in Geneva, Switzerland. He is the most celebrated Cuban Salsa teacher in the world.

● **Harold Jaffe** is busy promoting his recent book *Porn-anti-Porn* (reviewed in this issue) while working on a long text called "Rothko 66."

● **Alfred Jarry** (1875-1907) was one of the most imaginative and influential writers of the 19th century. His play *Ubu Roi,* a scatological parody of *Macbeth* launched his literary career and inspired the Theatre of the Absurd. *The Pope's Mustard-Maker,* excerpted in this issue, is available in paperback from Black Scat Books.

● **Jules Jouy** (1855-1897) was one of the most prolific poets of his time. He wrote over 3000 songs. both satirical and sentimental, with a penchant for anticlericalism and the macabre, and, after the Dreyfus affair, antisemitism. Many he performed himself at the Chat Noir. He also contributed verses and articles to many papers, wrote shadow plays, and started several papers of his own. His 1882 *Journal des merdeux* was suppressed for its unrelenting scatology. Poverty, overwork, and alcohol took their toll; in 1895 he was confined to a psychiatric hospital, dying there two years later at the age of 42.

● **Alexander Krivitskiy** is a photographer based in Kiev.

● **Olchar E. Lindsann** has published over 40 books of literature, theory, translation, and avant-garde history, most recently volume 3 of the ongoing series *Arthur Dies* on Luna Bisonte. His poems have appeared in *Otoliths, Lost & Found Times, Brave New Word*, and elsewhere, and he has performed sound poetry and lectured extensively in the US and the UK. He is the editor of mOnocle-Lash Anti-Press, whose catalog includes over 100 print publications of the contemporary and historical avant-garde, and of the periodicals *Rêvenance, The in-Appropriated Press*, and *Synapse*.

● **Joel Lipman** was appointed the first Poet Laureate of Lucas County, Ohio, in 2008. Emeritus professor at the University of Toledo, he founded Abracadabra Studio of Poetics. His poems appear in *Undocumented: Great Lakes Poets Laureates on Social Justice* (MSU Press, 2018).

● **Laura Mazzenga** is a writer and editor in the MFA program at San Diego State University.

● **Peter McAdam** is a UK based visual artist who explores the absurd through his ant-slick cartooning. Creator of the mash-up app iCodagraph, he seeks to subvert genres. Semi-reclusive he now spends his time as a coffee shop vampire.

● **Jim McMenamin** divides his time.

● **Doug Rice** is the author of *When Love Was, Here Lies Memory, An Erotics of Seeing, Das Heilige Buch der Stille, Faraway, So Close, Between Appear and Disappear, Dream Memoirs of a Fabulist, Blood of Mugwump*, and other books of fiction, photographs, and memoir. His work has appeared in numerous journals and anthologies, including *Zyzzyva, Gargoyle, Discourse*, and *Fiction International*. He was a Literary Fellow at the Akademie Schloss Solitude, Stuttgart, Germany, 2012-2014.

● **Arthur Rimbaud** and **Paul Verlaine** wrote the poem in this issue during the first bloom of their fraught relationship, at a meeting of the short-lived Zutiste group that congregated around Charles Cros at the Hôtel de l'Étranger in the months following the Paris Commune. The zutistes kept an album in which they composed playful collaborative poems, often far too experimental even for the avant-garde journals of their day; it is from this journal that their hyper-condensed, syntactically-fractured text here is drawn.

Jason E. Rolfe is the author of two novellas and two short story collections, including *An Inconvenient Corpse, An Archive of Human Nonsense*, and *Clocks*. He lives in Southwestern Ontario with his wife and daughter.

Paul Rosheim recently edited *Critics & My Talking Dog*, a selection of texts by Stefan Themerson, for Black Scat Books. Otherwise, he's engaged in writing short, informative notes, on a variety of subjects, which are left under rocks in the woods.

Doug Skinner has done numerous French translations for Black Scat Books, including works by Isidore Isou, Alphonse Allais, Pierre-Corneille Blessebois, Emile Goudeau, Charles Cros, and Alfred Jarry, as well as a collection of cartoons from *Le Chat Noir*. Black Scat has also published some lovely books of Skinner's own songs, stories, and cartoons. He is the only contributor to have voiced a Listerine radio spot, played ukulele on the Joe Franklin Show, played piano on the BBC, composed an MTV jingle, done a ventriloquism routine on a Martin Mull special, and lectured at the Visionary Art Museum in Baltimore.

Laurent Tailhade (1854-1919) was a tireless anarchist and Bohemian provocateur. His poetry was both savage and formally polished, often targeting the clergy and the middle class; collections include *Au Pays du mufle* (*In the Country of the Lout*, 1891) and *Imbéciles et gredins* (*Imbeciles and Scoundrels*, 1900). He was imprisoned for calling for the assassination of Tsar Nicolas II, once dumped his chamberpot on a religious procession, fought some thirty duels, and championed the consumption of opium. He famously defended terrorism as a "beautiful act," even after losing an eye in a bombing.

Gregory Wallace is a visionary poet and artist. He studied with surrealist author Nanos Valaoritis at San Francisco State University. His poetry and collages have appeared in *Black Scat Review, BlazeVOX, Clockwise Cat, Five 2 One* and *Danse Macabre*. A full length collection of his poetry, *Exile and Kingdom Come: Elysium*, was published in 2019.

Tom Whalen's books include *The President in Her Towers, The Straw That Broke, Elongated Figures, Winter Coat,* and *Dolls*. NYRB Classics will bring out his translation of Robert Walser's *Little Snow Landscape and Other Stories* in Spring 2020.

BLACK SCAT BOOKS

For more information, visit **BlackScatBooks.com**

ecstasy noun

ec·sta·sy | \ ˈek-stə-sē
plural **ecstasies**

Definition of *ecstasy*

1   **a**   : a state of being beyond reason and self-control

       b   *archaic* : SWOON

2   : a state of overwhelming emotion
     especially : rapturous delight

3   : TRANCE
     especially : a mystic or prophetic trance

4   *often capitalized* : a synthetic amphetamine analog $C_{11}H_{15}NO_2$ used illicitly for its mood-enhancing and hallucinogenic properties

Black
Scat Review

19

— theme —

e c s t a s y

Deadline:

March 31, 2020

Send to: blackscatbooks (AT) icloud (DOT) com

www.ingramcontent.com/pod-product-compliance
Lightning Source LLC
Chambersburg PA
CBHW030338020726
47493CB00004B/1316